Pink Lies

- a novel -

Haley Todd Kitts

Pink Lies is a work of fiction. Names, characters, places, and incidents either are the products of the author's imagination or are used fictitiously. Any resemblance to actual persons, living or dead, businesses, companies, events, or locales is entirely coincidental.

Set in Charleston, SC & New York City, New York

LIBRARY OF CONGRESS CATALOGING-IN-PUBLICATION-DATA
Names: Kitts, Haley Todd
Title: Pink Lies: a novel/ Haley Todd Kitts

ISBN-13:
978-1534909465
ISBN-10:
153490946X
ebook ASIN: A1JNAIHSSAXX27

Cover & Illustrations by Victoria Blanchard
Edit & Design by Jayce Williams
Formatting by Shanoff Formats

Table of Contents

to my wonderful mom,
for always telling me to sparkle and shine, baby!

One

"How to Save a Life"

You spend most of your life preparing for things that you probably wouldn't expect to happen. You go to school for the majority of your life studying, and practicing skills to prepare you for your career. Dumb long division, fractions, or how many atoms are required to form a molecule; unnecessary stuff that fills your brain, stuff you'll probably never use in the real world. *Trust* me on that. Then, to make things even more complicated, your mom makes you take an EMT class in high school so you can go to med school *"prepared"*. That's IF you ever go to med school. Not the route I took in life. I thought I wanted to be a doctor because I'm actually good at math and science. I *loved* biology and anatomy until they made me dissect a pig my senior year. That's where I drew the line. The EMT course obviously prepared me for college, but I didn't think I'd ever use my skills on anyone but maybe my own child one day.

This was actually the case for me *today*. Addison decided we needed one last trip to the beach for some serious sun drinking. The kind of day that blisters your skin and leaves you dehydrated because you forget the beer isn't *water*. Since summer is almost over I'm fine with getting that extra glow I needed to even out my tan lines before going back to school. I haven't been to the beach as much as I would like this summer because

I've been busy lifeguarding and teaching swim lessons at the pool in my neighborhood. Something else I was forced to do as a child; *swim team*. I'm an excellent swimmer no doubt, but after eighteen years of it you just burn out.

I offered to pick Addison up from her house downtown because my Jeep can hold more passengers than her tiny convertible. Sure, a convertible would probably be more fun to take to the beach, but you can't pile in all the chairs, coolers, and *cadets*. These "cadets" aren't allowed a ton of freedom during the school year, so it's nice for them to get a "Charleston Pass," also known as "leave" during the summer. The four of us do a lot of things together when they're allowed out of the *prison* cell they call college. You have no idea what it's like to be a student at the Citadel until you are friends with the inmates. They have it hard but they made the decision to go there. I always remind them, "You could've gone to Clemson." There's a book about it after all.

My mom had always hoped I would date Henry because he comes from such a fine (wealthy) family here in town. My mom grew up with his parents and attended the same private school together, so naturally she likes him. I adore Henry, he's a great guy, and he's really handsome, but we've told everyone for years we are *just* friends.

Conner is also from Charleston; we went to private school at Porter-Gaud, so we're buddies from a long time ago. He's practically the brother I never had growing up. I was hoping Addison would end up with one of the two because I know they are better options than anyone she's chosen to "date" lately.

"Are you guys ready to crush these beers and play some bocce ball?" Conner asked as he very loudly dumped a huge bag of ice from the gas station into the cooler and filled it with PBR's. The only beer we can afford and of course, I had to buy it because these yahoos aren't of age yet.

"I can't wait to beat you guys. I don't think I ever have. Maybe we can throw in a game of volleyball since bocce isn't my thing," I said as I turned up Hootie and opened my sunroof. Nothing says summer better than listening to loud music from the '90s with your best friends.

"I'm pretty sure I've beat all of you this summer which is kind of hilarious since all of you grew up by the beach and I didn't. Guess it's my *natural* athleticism I can thank," Addison boasted as she cracked open her first beer of the morning. This girl drinks like a fish. Better than any guy I'd ever met. She won the beer pong championship we went to on campus at the end of the semester. It made the guys butt-hurt they got out drank by a girl.

Henry called shotgun and DJ'd the songs for the duration of the trip. It didn't take us very long to get to Isle of Palms from downtown, probably thirty minutes with traffic. Henry's older cousin, Martha has a house on Carolina Boulevard that we always parked at during the summer. You can't even fathom the number of tourists here from April–October; parking is a nightmare. I told myself a long time ago that I would never pay for parking if I could help it. We are lucky Martha lets us come over all the time considering she's married with small children. Thankfully they were out of town today so we could go inside and use their kitchen to make lunch and rinse the sand off our feet when we got in. Their house is incredible. White tin roof, everything decorated with beautiful sea glass blue, beach cruisers in the garage, Ping-Pong table, and the most amazing fire pit. They have the ideal beach house that I pretend is my own quite frequently.

We spent most of the morning blistering in the sun and floating around in the ocean on these obnoxiously huge flamingo floats Conner's mom let us borrow. The bocce ball tournament had to come after we drank half the cooler's worth of beers according to Conner. He and Addison were the competitive ones in the group always wanting to win, taking no prisoners.

"Hey, why is that idiot snorkeling? He has to know we don't have any marine life worth seeing out here," Henry questions inquisitively while pointing at the man floating in the surf.

We all looked at him and glanced at each other with perplexed looks on our faces. Then it hit me. He isn't floating at all. He's *drowning.*

"He's not snorkeling!" I said as I run towards the ocean to the man in the water.

I ran as fast as my body would take me. My lifeguard training has paid off. I didn't have time to think about anything or look back to see what my friends were doing as I was running to this man. I didn't even think to look around for a lifeguard. It's almost off-season here so, there probably isn't one on duty. All I could think was how I would respond to this situation if the man were dead when I approached him. I would be devastated if I didn't catch him in time. I'm panicking, and now my heart is pounding.

I finally make it to the shore where he's floating aimlessly in the white caps of the ocean. The waves keep crashing over him like he's just a big rock stuck in the middle of the water. More like a huge boulder that won't move. I don't want to do anything too serious in the event he's paralyzed. It's sad to think, but it's possible he jumped off the Isle of Palms Pier to my left and drifted all the way here. I don't think many people come to the beach to commit suicide. Most people don't believe the beach to be a pernicious place; they find it to be their oasis.

I've never encountered something like this in my entire life. I've never seen anyone drown at the pool or the beach. I worked as a lifeguard the past six summers, and I've been lucky not to witness anything like this. I'm very scared for him as I attempt to pull him out of the surf. Dead weight is extremely hard to deal with in the water by yourself if you're wondering.

"Henry! Conner! I need help! Call 911, Addison!!" I demand as I'm still attempting to pull the man towards the beach.

I couldn't get him quite where I wanted until the boys came to my rescue. Literally everyone on the beach is staring at us, but nobody is coming to help. I can't believe people are just standing there taking pictures and videos on their phones as we try to save this man's life. It's sad to think they would rather get cool footage of a drowning man than offer their assistance.

"I checked his pulse, and it's barely there. I checked his eyes and his mouth; I think he needs to be flipped over, but I don't want to risk anything," I say as I try to check all his vitals. I know I need to perform CPR, but I'm nervous since this is my first time.

"I need an ambulance here NOW!"

"They're on their way," Addison reassures me as she stands by watching me place my hands on his chest.

I'm not used to seeing Addison in a state of panic or fear. She likes to put off this hard exterior, so nobody thinks she's weak, but she's really charismatic and kind. This is that moment I wasn't prepared for when I talk about life experiences. I never imagined I would have to perform CPR on anyone. Ever. I'm proud of myself for remembering how to do this considering I could barely stay awake during my lifeguard training. And I'm excited that I could help someone in need. I really should've gone into the medical field, but I chickened out. I love the adrenaline you get when you help someone like this. I feel guilty for feeling so exhilarated when a man is literally fighting for his life. It's a hard emotion to explain, but I think you get what I'm trying to say.

"Help me put him on his side, I need to get the water out of his lungs if I can," I tell the boys.

All the surrounding people as they watch me continue the chest compressions are asking me questions, "Is he going to live? Are you going to save him? Is he even alive?" "How about all of you just back the hell away from Scarlett, she needs space to do this!" says Addison in a very commanding tone.

As soon as the water starts pouring out the side of his mouth, he starts to cough a little and seems to be alert to the situation.

"Sir? Are you ok? Can you hear me?"

I don't get a response because he looks like he's going to code. Thankfully the EMS was pulling onto the beach as this was happening because it's getting out of hand. I can only do so much with the knowledge I have. They drove right to where we are and asked me a ton of questions about what happened and what had I done to help so far. I didn't want to put myself in a predicament, so I kind of just backed away. They put him on a stretcher and started to perform more CPR.

Naturally, the day I want to relax with my friends at the beach a man needs to be saved from drowning. This kind of thing only happens to *me*. I was rattled for the next hour or so. I didn't know what to do or what to say. I'm worried for the guy because he's alone and doesn't have any belongings. Nobody saw him on the beach earlier that morning.

The *one* day I decide to wear this obnoxious bikini with tassels on the front, I save a man's life. I had a lot of people come up to me asking me about the incident. I'm starting to feel somewhat like a hero. I like the feeling, but the attention is starting to stress me out.

"Y'all want to get lunch at the Wind Jammer? I could *really* use a stronger drink right about now," Henry asked the group.

"I can't even think about food right now. I feel emotionally depleted after what just happened. Y'all go ahead without me. I think I just need to head home."

I didn't get why I was feeling this way. I thought I would be happy that I helped the man, but I couldn't stop thinking why would he do this to himself if he were committing suicide.

Once I'm home, I take a shower, alternating between hot and cold so

I can shake this feeling of nervousness. My mom is still at work and my sister Savannah is out with a friend. I'm thankful for some peace and quiet so that I can try and think this over. I want to tell them, but I'm not quite ready to relive it yet. I crawl into my bed and turn my phone off so I can rest well.

Nearly five hours passed, and I finally start to wake up from what felt like four days. I hear a loud voice in my room screaming at me to wake up.

"Scarlett!! Wake up! Is this you?" Savannah asks as she shows me a picture on her Facebook.

"Oh my gosh. Yes. Where did you find this?"

"It's all over my newsfeed. I couldn't figure out if it were you or someone that looked like you. I remember you have that swimsuit, though; kind of hard to mistake for someone else."

"How is it all over your feed? How is this on here?"

"My friend posted it, and I saw a bunch of other posts where people were talking about the incident outside the Wind Jammer today."

"Don't show mom yet. I need to collect my thoughts."

"Well, are you going to explain what the heck is going on here?"

I spent the next half hour rehashing the events from this morning to my baby sister. Savannah's jaw was dropped for nearly the entire conversation. Having to explain this to her made me realize how horrific the accident really was. Of course, Savannah's first call of action is post a status tagging me saying that her sister is "the" hero who saved the man's life. I want to call the hospital, but I have no idea where they took him. I assume MUSC downtown Charleston considering his critical condition.

I decide I should probably check my Facebook as well to see what kind of shit storm I'm about to be in. No doubt I find my wall blown up with people asking me if I'm the girl in the green bikini. I didn't realize people cared so much about these kinds of things. I was under the impression that kids my age were too absorbed with themselves and their electronics.

I finally turn my phone on after having it off all afternoon to see I have several voicemails from numbers I didn't recognize. I listen to all of them, and as I suspected, the first is my mother who got wind of this before I could even explain it. She isn't happy that I didn't call to tell her. Then, I hear a message from a local news anchor wanting to do a story and interview me for her piece. I don't want to draw that kind of attention to myself but if it will help me know more about the victim's condition I'll do it.

I call the reporter because I'm curious what she wants from me. I'm not excited to have to be behind the camera at all. She told me she wanted to do a story on the brave girl who saved the drowning man in front of the Wind Jammer on Isle of Palms. I told her I would do it but only if I could get information about the victim.

The next day I met the reporter outside the Wind Jammer to conduct the interview. She told me that this was the type of story that can't be kept a secret. She said it was too heartwarming not to tell the entire city of Charleston about the selfless girl who saved a man's life. I didn't care about the formalities I just answered her questions, and she made me feel like I deserved a gold medal or something. It lasted about twenty minutes, and I realized quickly that I didn't want to go into acting. She said I did a fabulous job, and it would be on a local news channel later that night.

She told me that the victim's name was Jeff, and he has a wife and three boys that live in Atlanta. Apparently they were able to ID him at the hospital and got in contact with her. Although he narrowly escaped drowning, his pulmonary system was severely compromised in the accident. He has had multiple episodes of his heart stopping, each time requiring CPR to revive him. He has had surgery to fuse and stabilize his neck, but he definitely has a long road ahead of him.

I'm heartbroken hearing of this tragic news. I was hoping he would come out of this unscathed. She told me it was possible the family would reach out to me to help grasp the incident better. I didn't mind talking to them; I wanted to know more about Jeff and what kind of guy he is.

My news story went viral across the nation. There were news stations I had never even heard of talking about it. I didn't know how something so small like this could become so significant. Everyone in town recognized me from the news and wanted to give me hugs for the next month. My professors treated me with a new kind of respect that I didn't have in the past. Everyone was proud of me for saving Jeff. All I could think of was the condition he was in; how will he pull through?

Two

Two Years Later

"Shots, shots!!" demanded all the drunken girls eagerly lined up around the bar clapping and cheering us on hoping for us to partake in their fun. They want us to take our tequila the *proper* way: salt on your hand, suck the lime and take it back like a champ. Drinking tequila shots at the end of the night became a trend this summer with my partner in crime, Addison Webster. The music is literally deafening at this place; the base is shaking the floor. The only lighting up here is at the bar, and the white twinkling Christmas lights on the palm trees. The kind of ambiance you want at a bar so we are getting pretty *buzzed* at this point.

"I can't take any more shots tonight, or I'm going to puke right over this rooftop directly onto someone's head!" I said it in a serious tone trying to convey my point.

"Listen, we are recent college graduates without jobs so we should take advantage of all the hot guys tonight and have fun. Stop being a buzzkill, Scarlett." She said as she was slurping down a vodka soda that she just received from a guy across the bar. Probably some fool coming from a wedding earlier tonight hoping to get lucky.

"I understand you're trying to live in the moment here, and I appreciate that I really do, but I feel super dizzy. We've been going out every Thursday-Saturday since we graduated three months ago, and my liver is shutting down," I said as I put my very long hair into a braid to prepare myself for the toilet debauchery that's sure to ensue later.

"Ok, *one* last dance with tuxedo guy. He just bought me this drink; I think I owe him since he got me *Grey Goose* instead of that cheap Smirnoff shit that burns going down. You can chug some water and figure out how we are getting home, and I'll be back before the song is over."

The fact of the matter is- if Addison were ready to leave, I would have to go *hell* or *high water*. She doesn't take no for an answer, but I'm apparently a "pushover." She knows I've been really stressed because I've been interviewing for jobs since April that haven't amounted to anything special. I'm sure she just wants to take my mind off the real problem here: I'm not going to get any of the jobs I want with my wrap-sheet; my wrap- sheet being my shitty, underachiever, loser-ass resume.

"Ok, did you request the Uber?" Addison asked as she put her wedges back on after having them off half the night to dance. It's shocking she doesn't have permanently black feet from being barefoot at bars.

"Yea, it's on its way now-it says four minutes en-route."

We close our tabs and stumble our way onto the elevator. We're on the penthouse level of this swanky hotel called The Market Pavilion Hotel that has a rooftop bar. There's even a pool here that you can lay out during the day if you're a guest at the hotel. I'm shocked that nobody has tumbled right in after too many rum and cokes. It serves mainly as a place for wild girls to go with their bachelorette groups or sorority parties. Meaning there was likely to be a cornucopia of hot guys, so we didn't mind the sea of Lilly Pulitzer and Vineyard Vines.

The view is incredible; you can basically see the all of downtown Charleston at night. This bar offers a full campus of perks; therefore, we continue to come regularly. We *kind of* got kicked out of the bar we really liked, called Mad River. The place used to be a church, but the owners turned it into a bar; seems pretty blasphemous if you ask me. Addison got in a bit of a quarrel with this sorority girl who was trying to hit on the guy she liked at the time. Addison thought it would be ok to throw a drink in her face, it wasn't-we got escorted out by a bouncer. Needless to say, we don't go there anymore. The bartenders knew us well, so we got a lot of free drinks. Perhaps we were over served that night.

I did feel better after chugging three glasses of ice water, but my head is pounding now. The kind of pounding that leads to the room spinning uncontrollably. I just want to go home because I'm supposed to be at church tomorrow morning with my grandparents. They said if they let me crash at their house downtown, I have to try and go with them in the morning.

I *would* stay at Addison's house, but her place is equivalent to a high-end brothel. More like a nasty frat house being that she lives with three other soccer players that aren't the pinkest of girls. They have their lease until July, so unfortunately, they are still there. Addison isn't one for caring about her house's cleanliness. I'm a bit of a germophobe, and I like order, so I just stay at my grandparent's in their carriage house on the Battery. Addison picked me up there earlier tonight. She left her car across the street so she could leave whenever she wanted once we got back without them knowing.

We wait outside the hotel like a couple of cheap hookers for our ride. I never wondered what it would feel like to be in a *Pretty Woman* situation until right now. I say that because who else wears mini-skirts, with these kinds of heels, their hair up, with their makeup halfway running down their face sitting on the curb at two in the morning? *Hookers*. Not really the Vivian Ward kind either. She was pretty classy.

Addison told me when we graduated that I need to get the stick out of my ass before I start the real world. She said it would be a rude awakening for me if I can't loosen up. I know I need to, but I found that I always had to be the responsible party in the situation. My sister is much younger than I am. My parents got divorced when I was sixteen, so I had to grow up faster than I wanted. I sometimes feel I was robbed of my childhood.

We talked as we waited for the car to arrive and start scheming for my next interview. That is *if* I could get one. Addison is always one to push the envelope. She isn't a bad person or a mean person; she just likes to see how far she can push the envelope.

After we had gathered our shoes and our purses, we got in the Uber and headed towards the other side of King Street. Addison thought she could stay the night and leave in the morning without my grandparents seeing or hearing her. She wasn't about to be guilted into going to church with a hangover.

"I have a great idea for you, Scar," she mumbled as she rested her head on my lap in the backseat. Addison requested one of the nice "select" vehicles as usual. Glad we requested this on *her* dime and not mine.

"I can only imagine what that idea might be."

"I think you should fabricate your resume a lil bit. A white lie isn't as bad as a real lie. It's just deception," she said.

"Now what would make you think I would have the balls to do that?" I was curious how she thought I could pull this off.

As I listen to her plan, it actually sounds like a good idea. I don't want to break any laws, but I figure it's only bad *if* I get caught. Addison said it was better to ask forgiveness than permission in this kind of situation. I'm starting to think she's right. I don't know how I'm going to land a job working at a magazine syndicate if I don't alter my resume just *slightly*.

After we got back, we quietly went up the stairs of the carriage house like a couple of sneaky teenagers and got ready for bed. For me, that meant taking a full-length shower to rid myself from the smoky, cheap-liquor smell. Addison was fine throwing a t-shirt on and hopping right into bed without washing an inkling of makeup off her face. I, on the other hand, cannot sleep feeling and smelling disgusting with this humidity we have going on.

I get out of the piping hot shower, and Addison is on my Mac with a *sinister* grin on her face. I'm concerned she's setting up some profile for Tinder or something. Addison probably thinks a boyfriend would help solve my problem; that I should just marry some trust fund baby of one of the wealthy family's here in town. Maybe she will fall asleep soon. I was wrong. Apparently two in the morning is no big deal to her.

Addison woke up early because she's trying to avoid being spotted by my grandparents. I'm kind of in the same boat as her; I want to avoid sitting in a sixty-minute bore fest where I would have to try and keep my eyes open. I decide it would be ok to sneak out with her since they didn't even know we were there. I made the bed with precise hospital corners just as my grandmother had it before we got here. We check the room like a CSI crime scene for any of our belongings and left down the back stairs hoping nobody would see us.

Addison parked on the street diagonally in front of their house so they wouldn't know we came over. I felt bad lying to the people who literally treat me like *gold*. My grandparents give me everything and more; seems like this lie is already starting to turn me into a criminal mastermind. I can see how the rest of my life will unfold from here.

"Damnnnn! A parking ticket? How in the world did that happen on a Sunday?" Said Addison in a perturbed voice as she crumpled her ticket and threw it in her Prada bag.

The look of disdain was painted all over her face. She didn't like when she was wrong. *Ever.*

"You aren't allowed to park in front of a fire hydrant, no matter what day it is you moron."

I'm not supposed to find her wrong doing so humorous. It was always funny to me when she broke the law that she was supposed to uphold as a future attorney. For a girl trying to get into law school, Addison sure knew how to *bend* the law.

We sped off in her little silver BMW convertible that her parent's got her for having impeccable grades. She probably deserved it the way she studied for her classes and tests like it was her job for the past four years. Probably why she wants to go out so much because her life is about to be over once, she gets into law school. I wouldn't know what it feels like to be in her position. I'm still living at home, working as a hostess at the Daniel Island Grille, most commonly referred to as "the DIG" to the locals around here.

She dropped me off at home, and I broke down and drank some grape Pedialyte that I bought at the CVS on the way here. If you want to cure a hangover quickly, just drink that nasty ass childhood elixir. You'll feel brand new within the hour. It's disgusting and might make your symptoms worse for a few minutes, but the results are worth it. You'll feel great the rest of the day.

I went to my room since my mom and sister was sleeping. It's only eight in the morning-I figure I can just sleep until they wake up around noon or so.

I open all the shutters to the bright sunshine beaming in my room and warmth and close them immediately because my eyes are in no way ready for the brightness. I literally feel like a vampire drained of blood. I slam the shutters to darken the blinding sun and rest peacefully for the next six hours.

Three

East Side, West Side, Dilly-Dang-Dong

I spent the entire summer after graduation trying to get jobs on the West coast and East coast and every *other* coast working at a popular magazine conglomerate. Elle, Seventeen, Vogue, and Glamour; you name it. I didn't land any of the jobs I wanted. I had several interviews at local places in my hometown of Charleston, South Carolina. They were only obligatory interviews because my mom, Kate Riley, works for a powerful senator that's soon to be on Capitol Hill. I literally *loathe* the idea of settling for the small local newspaper writing about all the upcoming million dollar weddings of the debutants I went to private school with my whole life. I'm also not the type of girl who takes a job because someone is doing my 'mommy' a favor. I don't think so! I knew the only way to actually work for a real magazine writing about real topics was to change a few things on my resume. I didn't see it as a huge crime when my thoughts weren't lucid, but now I feel convicted about it since I'm sober and know better.

Some things are just better off left unsaid; especially when it comes to telling your parents who think they have raised the most wonderful and *honest* daughter. When my mom asked me how the interviews were going, I told her they were going just fine if getting interviews were the same as getting the job as she opened the door to my room. I spent a lot of time in my room the past few months at my desk applying to jobs that weren't going anywhere.

"Scarlett, I think it's time we hire a head hunter to get you that job you really deserve," she said while holding my laundry basket full of nicely folded clothes; perks of living at home.

"Mom, I don't want to waste any more time hoping they can find me the *'perfect job'* when I've already wasted a *perfectly* good summer sitting in my room. I've applied to every job posting on LinkedIn that I come across. I'm over it."

"If you need any help revamping your resume just let me know, honey," my mom said sweetly. That is when I truly felt the remorse set in. I can feel my chest tightening; similar to heartburn because I knew what I was doing was totally wrong and probably identity theft in some states. Maybe worse.

After my mom had made the comment about helping with my resume, I wondered if she had a clue as to what I was doing. Moms have this weird premonition or sixth sense when their child is up to something naughty. Growing up active in church, my grandparents and Sunday school teachers always taught me that lying is a sin and that all sins were equal. We don't go to church as much as we used to when my parents were together. Mom always says that just because you go to church doesn't mean you're going to heaven. She liked to use the analogy, "just because you're in a garage doesn't make you a car," it makes more sense, as I get older.

It's too bad that my father, Roger, didn't pay attention in worship service on Sunday's. His lies to my mom over and over led to their divorce after she caught him cheating with another woman in town named, Naomi Meyer. She's a plastic surgeon that fixed small breast all day for a living. I guess he got tired of my mom working on political campaigns all the time; spending all those late nights working with young lobbyist trying to pass laws on abortion and same-sex marriage.

My dad didn't grow up Southern at all. In fact, he's from Malibu, California on the other side of the "planet" as my grandfather says. My mom met him during undergrad at Pepperdine University. They had a political science class together and were partners in a group project. My grandparents didn't want her going out West, but she had never left the South before college. So, almost by default she fell in love with my dad her senior year, and they got married a year and a half later here in Charleston. My grandparents were disappointed when Kate Riley, the South of Broad, *Southern Belle*, married the *liberal hippy* surfer dude from Malibu.

My dad isn't the moneymaker in the family either so that's unsettling for my mom's parents as well. He's a freelance detective for several local police departments here in Charleston. My grandparents knew they were doomed from the beginning of their relationship because money always causes marital issues. Their marriage lasted because of my sister and me. They are good parents to us, but bad spouses sadly.

I decided I would keep my little resume charade between Addison and myself for as long as I could. I was merely taking a page out of her book. Plus, I haven't done anything with it yet; it's just saved to my desktop staring back at me.

Addison is the type of girl who you want to go to bars and parties with, but you were afraid to tell her your deepest and darkest secrets. At least that's how I felt about her at first. Of course, things have changed. She's a great girl with a big heart, and she comes from a wonderful family. I met the Webster's once when we went to her house in Washington D.C. for Spring Break. Addison was my roommate in college my freshman year. They placed her with me because we were *really* compatible apparently. I learned to trust her after she went through a huge breakup with this douche named Brody the first semester of school. She confided all these major details about him mentally and sometimes physically abusing her. She isn't one to divulge that kind of information so I knew she trusted me. Therefore, I should trust her too. After that, I felt really close to her. I don't think that says very much about my character, but I thought her honesty was really brave.

I decide to call Addison and see if she would convince me not to submit my new resume to all these online applications.

"If you don't do this you'll *always* wonder what it could have been like working your dream job. Instead, you'll end up marrying someone in town you met at the grocery store while buying cheap box wine that works as a P.E. teacher or something lame. You'll have six kids and drive a mini- van to all their karate classes."

"I'm going to send it into a few places as soon as I can figure out all the crimes I'm committing by creating a fraudulent resume." I did actually look up all the crimes I could have been committing by altering my resume just slightly. It seems like I'll only be in trouble "if" I get caught and it wasn't a serious crime. I'm hoping that these companies don't do the thorough background checks that my mom is always telling me about when they hire new people for their campaigns. I don't plan on changing my name or anything drastic-just a few extracurricular activities and maybe a better GPA. I will just take my LinkedIn profile down for a while and put privacy settings on all my social media.

My mom lets me live at home rent-free as long as I helped volunteer for the campaign this summer. I *loathe* politics, but she let me create ads and flyers so I wouldn't have to get my hands dirty in the drama of it all.

I worked as a hostess at the sports bar on the island to make some extra money and get out of the house occasionally. She also gives me a weekly allowance like a little child in middle school. I'm surprised that I don't have a chore chart with gold stars. I shouldn't complain because it's actually a really nice gesture that she doesn't have to do. I help out around the house, babysit, and cook dinner every night for my sister, Savannah. She's seven years younger than me making her fifteen years old and just annoying enough because she couldn't be trusted alone yet with the opposite sex. Not to mention she can't drive. I knew I didn't want to be doing this well into the fall months so I decide I will finish my resume tonight.

After dinner and making sure Savannah was good to go, I went to 'work out' if you could even call it that. We have a home gym in the basement. It only has a treadmill and some free weights; nothing special. A place people usually go to get in shape; for me, it is merely a place I go to escape and procrastinate doing things I should be doing. My mom had this built after my dad, and she separated. It was her goal to look better than Naomi. We even put in a little sauna big enough for two people to go in at a time. I think sweating out my frustration tonight would be quite cathartic.

When I got out of the shower, I looked in the mirror and noticed I'm starting to get crow's feet around my eyes. The stress this summer has caused me is making me prematurely age. I'm not getting any younger, and this job predicament is getting to me, so I finish my resume and send it in.

I've been on several trips out West this summer spending my life savings to go on interviews that amounted to, "We were very impressed with your credentials, but we have moved on with a candidate we feel better suited for this position. We've saved your resume for future applications. Please feel free to apply to other positions in the future." Probably the automated response they send to every candidate not worthy of the position.

I don't think I will receive an email like that after the new and improved Scarlett Hanes is introduced. I'm tired of being dumped by companies so I just add a few extra things to my resume that will help me stand out.

I add "Campaign Assistant for Senator Tom Wellington," which isn't a total lie I did work for my mom but in a looser sense.

I'm now, according to this, CofC's ADPI chapter president; I figure being involved in something that stood out is important. These were the girls I never liked because they all seemed superficial, and dated the entire population of comb-over, loafer wearing frat boys at school. I think for some reason putting this on my resume is more of an inside joke to myself. I must say, though, all the girls I know that were in a sorority have really good jobs now. Apparently it looks good to have been involved in marathon drinking events and socials at expensive country clubs.

I made myself Assistant editor-in- chief to one of Charleston's local newspaper and magazines so that they knew I could write. Again, not a total lie because I did write articles for local magazines for one of my classes. A few got submitted my last year of college. If they look that up, they will find it with my name attached to it.

Lastly, I put the semesters I got Dean's list, which was almost every semester of college because I have a 3.75 GPA now. I didn't want to give myself the perfect 4.0 because how would I be able to achieve everything else on top of school with that kind of GPA? Can't be too perfect of course.

The positions I was applying for wanted local residents of NYC, and I'm not living there yet as you know. It's not that big of a deal; people lie about where they live all the time. They all say they need to hire immediately, so I'm hoping this won't be a long, arduous process.

I need an address for my resume, or they will just toss mine out before getting to the education section. The only person I can think of off the top of my head that lives in NYC is Addison's older sister, Claire. She is three years older than Addison and me, so it doesn't seem too old but just old enough that she probably thinks she's more mature than we are. I text Addison to ask what Claire's address is and ask if I could *maybe* use her address *temporarily* on my resume.

"I don't think Claire would mind," says Addison in her very brief text-so brief that I wonder if she really would mind. I had to take that chance. I said I only need it to land an interview, and then I will obviously change it when I get the job.

"Sure, go ahead but I'm not asking Claire. Just do it and we can worry about it later," Addison chimed when I got her text fifteen minutes later, longer than her usual response time of four point five seconds.

I start searching for jobs online in the fashion writing industry. I did minor in art, so I have always been interested in clothing and jewelry. I worked at a boutique on King Street throughout college called Copper Penny. They sell high-end designer clothing at a *really* steep price that hardly anyone my age could afford. Who pays $300 for a pool cover up? I got a discount, so luckily I was able to dress nicely for the most part. Sometimes the manager would suggest I wear the jewelry they sold during my shift to look the part.

I knew I didn't want to work in the relationships or beauty segments of the magazine. All types of unappealing jobs to me I had interviewed for this summer with other small publications that you've probably never heard of in your life. I knew a long time ago that I had a 'passion for fashion,' as dumb as that sounds.

I open my resume that I saved to my desktop an hour ago and did a once over *one more time* checking for any imperfections. It looks great, so I decide to take the plunge and send some emails with my resume attachment and a few letters of recommendation that *were* actually real. Perks of my mom knowing people in high places! I don't like accepting favors from anyone, but sometimes you have to in order to get ahead in this life.

Now to play the waiting game-the *paralyzing* process that big companies go through to make you jump at every email or phone call with the area code from their location. They usually know immediately after reviewing your information if they want you to come in, but they wait it out just to keep you guessing for as long as possible. Of course, I'll be the one who has to wait on pins and needles for two months.

Four

Invisible Crown

The way I feel is *sheepish*. I'm scared because I wondered all the *what-ifs* that could happen if they found out I lied, "a little" on several parts of my resume. Surely it doesn't take six weeks to do a background check on my information. I have to think that they're just busy working on a deadline or something since fashion week was quickly approaching. This kind of company spends months leading up to fashion week trying to prepare the best segments possible.

They probably have so many applicants to comb through that I got lost in a pile of maybes or straight up NOPE.

The first few weeks I was really optimistic because I felt good about my applications. I even feel like Addison, and I are on better terms since asking for Claire's address. She was as excited as I was in the first few weeks. Now, we were both freaking out a bit.

I call Addie hoping she would join me for some window-shopping on King Street and get dinner/drinks-*many* drinks. I need some liquid therapy if we're being honest. She came over and picked me up, and we went downtown. She always had the top down to her car, but especially now because it's the screen porch to hell weather you often hear about with this city. I love riding with the top down, but it really messes your hair up with the *sticky* humid air. Addison could wear her luscious, straight brunette hair in a ponytail, with a baseball hat and take it down when we got out, and it would look perfect. My very long, wavy blonde hair, would get tangled and look like I just wrestled a couple of pigs. I just learned to braid it to the side and get over it.

After perusing the unorganized racks at Forever21 and trying on push up bras at Victoria Secret that constantly deceive men, (Victoria's real secret), we decide to go Taco Boy for dinner. One thing was clear to me; I needed some strawberry margaritas and queso that have more calories than my breakfast and lunch combined to make me feel better. The servers practically expected us to come since we went almost every *Thirsty-Thursday* this summer for half price margaritas. Now that summer is over they aren't on special, but we still go every now and then to keep the tradition alive.

"Do you think we should toast to you waiting on the interview and *me* getting into law school?" Addison announced in a pleasant manner as she scarfed down the chips and salsa on the table.

"You got in?!?! I thought you didn't hear back for another month or two?"

"I applied for early admissions, and I just found out. I leave for Georgetown in two weeks."

"That's amazing news! I'm so happy for you, Addie. I know you're so excited and proud you got into your top choice law school."

"I'm sad to be moving away from you without you knowing your fate. I know you're going to get that phone call or email *really soon*," she said as she motioned our server for more drinks changing the subject.

We took our margaritas and raised them up for a toast for Addison getting into Georgetown and for me not losing hope yet. After only three margaritas since they weren't half priced, we decided to call it a night. I don't think my bank account can handle many more therapy nights downtown. I really need to hear from one of those companies, like *yesterday*.

After we paid our bill and walked to her car, we reminisced on our summer. Addison and I were sort of in the same boat up until right now-a very *rocky* boat that you want to get off of immediately because you were getting seasick.

Just as we approach the Ravenel Bridge, my mom text me to come home and have a "girl's night in," exactly what I need tonight. It's like she read my mind. I'm happy for my best friend, but I feel a pang of sadness that she's about to live out her dream, and I'm just the loser who lives with my mom and my younger sister who only has $465.47 in her bank account.

Addison dropped me off on Daniel Island where I live with my 'roommates' and told me she would see me before she left for Georgetown. I know she will be busy getting organized and moved out for school. I considered going back to school to get my master's, but I didn't like school much when I was there, much less another two years of agony.

I walk through the door, and my mom and Savannah are painting their nails and watching *27 Dresses*.

"Scarlett, have you heard from any companies yet?" my mom asked.

Of course, she would ask that after the night I had. I told her no I have not heard yet, but I'm hoping I will this week. My sister offered to paint my nails, which is surprisingly sweet of her. She isn't one to be affectionate towards me. I think she is jealous of the relationship I have with my mom since we were closer in age. We had a nice evening watching mindless chick flicks and eating food with high-fat content and no remorse.

The next morning I woke up late with what felt like a horrific migraine because I had consumed those margaritas and half a bottle of chardonnay with my mom- perks of being twenty-one and your mom being a wine-o. I open the shutters as I always do to find it rainy with ominous looking clouds outside. I love these kinds of days, so I don't feel guilty about not leaving my bedroom.

I grab my phone on my nightstand and unplug it to see three missed calls and thirty-four emails in my inbox. The missed calls are from my mother, sister, and some unknown caller. I ignore those and skip social media to check my inbox. I scroll through all of the unwanted email subscriptions from various places like Nordstrom Rack and Expedia. I finally get to the top and see the subject to be "Interview Opportunity for Scarlett Hanes" and it's hard for me not to freak out as my eyes are seeing something I've wanted to see for months. I open the email and see the following reading it out loud to myself:

Good Morning Scarlett,

I hope this email finds you well. The hiring team at Cosmopolitan Magazine was very impressed with your application that you sent in August. We would love to sit down with you to further discuss the opportunity as Junior Editor for the fashion segment of our magazine.

We see that you currently reside in NYC, so we would love to see you tomorrow at two in the afternoon if that suits your schedule.

Please let us know as soon as you can so we can set something up for you and our hiring manager, Nicole Ashley.

Sincerely,

Susan Williams, HR Director

Cosmopolitan Magazine

300 W. 57th St

New York, NY 10019

Shit! Holy shit! I just got offered the interview of a lifetime at Cosmo!!!

Wait...I didn't apply to Cosmopolitan? How did this happen? I can only think of one possible thing: *Addison*. I give her a quick phone call to see if I was right.

"I must've done that after we went out that one night. Whoops! Hope you're not too angry with me!"

She seemed to be giggling as I was telling her. This isn't funny. I had no idea what resume she submitted. I guess I have to hand it to her for actually going through with it. I shouldn't be too mad; I did get an interview with my favorite magazine after all.

I don't even know what to do except panic because they expect me in NYC *tomorrow* at two in the afternoon, and I'm at home *very*, very far away from Claire's address. I check my bank account, and I have just enough to fly round-trip and maybe get food if I'm lucky. I book an early morning flight that gets into JFK at eleven A.M. after a connection in D.C. The connecting flight has a forty-seven-minute layover, so that shouldn't affect my arrival time. I book it with zero hesitations and call my mom right away to give her the news. Probably should've asked for the money but I didn't want her to talk me out of this crazy plan I concocted.

She picks up after several what seemed like very long rings and tells me she can't talk that she's walking into an *important* meeting. She always said her meetings were *important,* so I didn't even blink this time. I had a long list of people I wanted to tell because this is the proudest of myself I've been in years. Even though I embellished my resume a bit, I'm really proud. I'm also a little freaked out thinking of how I'm going to keep spinning this lie tomorrow in my interview. I knew I would have to do some research tonight and tomorrow at the airport.

"Mom, I'm packing as we speak to fly to NYC in the morning because your girl got an interview at Cosmopolitan Magazine!"

"Wow, Scarlett, honey that is so incredible! I'm proud of you. Tonight we will have a healthy dinner and get you squared away for your trip. I can't wait to hear all about it," she said.

She actually sounded very enthused considering she was going into her "important meeting" that was apparently not so important.

I booked my trip so that I'd be back in Charleston by late tomorrow evening. I didn't want to pay for a hotel. Correction: I couldn't afford a hotel. I'm not about to ask Claire because chances of me needing to stay there very soon for more than a night were pretty high.

I spent the next few hours trying on all of my interview appropriate clothes, but nothing seemed good enough for Cosmo. I want to sit in the middle of my floor and have a Tasmanian devil whirlwind. I just want to scream very loudly because the lie I told is already spinning its web. I finally decide on a navy skirt suit my mom got me at Brooks Brothers when I graduated. She even took me to the tailor so it would fit properly. She told me that classic clothes like this never go out of style. I decide that a girl from South Carolina should wear pearls, so I add them to the number.

It's approaching midnight, and I have to be at the airport at 7:30 A.M. for my 9:30 A.M. flight. I can't sleep. I feel like I'm going to throw up all night long as I lie in bed and look up at the ceiling. I know I'm not hungry, but my stomach aches with a hollow feeling.

I keep checking my email to make sure they haven't cancelled my interview. I would be absolutely livid and very screwed if they cancelled last minute because of an emergency or something. Delta doesn't refund flights for *liars*.

I finally fell asleep and woke up to the loudest and most annoying alarm that I found on my phone last night. I wasn't about to miss my flight so I could sleep. I put on workout clothes because I'm afraid I will wrinkle my suit. I'm hoping to have time to change into it when I arrive at JFK.

My mom had coffee prepared and a granola bar for me. She took me to the airport and dropped me off with a kiss and a go get 'em attitude speech. Her support means a lot. It also means a lot that she didn't question how I got this interview. She must *actually* believe in me. More than I believe in myself apparently. I can't spend the day rehashing my decision to lie and decision to be someone I'm not really sure of. Hell, I don't even know what's on the resume they have so I will pretend my printer was broken, and I couldn't bring a copy. That probably won't make a very good first impression but what choice do I have. Geez, Addison!

It's time for me to put on my *invisible crown,* and rock out this interview. "Sparkle and shine, baby!" That's what my mom always told me.

Five

Strangers Are Just Friends   You've Never Met

There are few things in life that I feel truly speak to me. I love to cook; it has been a passion of mine since my dad left the house. He used to be the one doing the cooking because my mother certainly can't. I learned a lot from him, and the queen of the kitchen, Barefoot Contessa. Then magazines. I love to read mindless magazines much like the one I'm interviewing for this afternoon. I find reading about other people's problems in the relationship segments to be cathartic since my relationships haven't amounted to anything in my twenty-two years on this planet. Last, but not least, New York City.

I live in the dirty south, or "Chuck Town," as they call it here, and I've always wanted to live in the Big Apple. My mom took Savannah and me when we were eighteen and eleven for the first time. I was at the age where I wanted to go to cool clubs and bars and check out the art museums and Savannah wanted to buy American Girl Dolls and see Broadway shows. It's been a struggle for the Hanes family to go on vacations for as long as I can remember because of my sister and our age difference. Something about New York was so enticing. The street smells, the constant people watching, the shopping and so many incredible sites. I knew I could probably land a great job writing here since every major magazine existed out of NYC. The amount of people in the streets or on the subway didn't even bother me. The traffic annoyed the hell out of me at home, but NYC felt very different and exciting in a good way.

Going to board my plane I grab my Tory Burch bag that I bought this summer with graduation money from my *very* wealthy and generous grandparents, and my briefcase that's housing my writing samples that are *actually* real. I'm holding my hang up bag with my suit hoping they will let me on with three personal items. Luckily they did. Another thing that I found very lucky was the seat next to me is empty, and that never happens. It's the perfect place to put my hang up bag that I had planned on ditching before my interview; just one of those flimsy plastic ones from Target. Today is starting out swimmingly if I must say. I usually have pretty decent luck, which will hopefully follow me into my interview later. As we take off, I'm thinking about what the person or people who are interviewing me will be wearing. What will they look like, what will they ask? I did my due-diligence at my gate before this and looked through the company directory online hoping to put some names with faces. The lady I think I'm interviewing with is Nicole Ashley, the hiring manager of Cosmopolitan Magazine that Susan mentioned in her email. It's possible they will just put me with three people that have a similar position to what I'm interviewing for and I'll have to come back the next day or two to meet with Nicole. That happened to me the last time I interviewed at home for a local newspaper. That's going to be a big problem for me since I'm flying home tonight. I hope they aren't trying to hire this week because I will be homeless unless I beg my grandfather for a loan. I don't want to milk them dry.

The plane has landed- I'm exhausted and can't stop yawning. I realize I only had like, four hours of sleep, and I'm only a few hours away from the biggest moment of my adult life. I decide to grab an espresso at the nearby coffee stand. The line is about ten people deep and ten waiting for their drink order, so I left and went to my gate. I should just take this time and put my suit on and touch up my make-up and hair. I didn't think I would get it too wrinkled since it's a short flight. I flip my hair under the hand dryer and ditched my hang up bag and walked towards my gate. I'm glad I skipped that line because the plane was actually boarding as I walked up.

I hand the attendant my ticket and board my flight with sheer anxiety knowing I was about to be in the city. This time, I'm not so lucky and got stuck sitting next to a mother and her crying infant. I look around hoping to find an open seat or sit with someone who doesn't sound like my alarm clock this morning. The flight's completely full. The lady decides she's going to talk to me when the last thing I want to do is listen to her baby cry and talk to her about my life. I never like small talk on a plane; nobody does-it's awkward. You end up divulging major details of your life and never even catch their name. People love to self-disclose their personal life to strangers. I don't get it. You're supposed to sit tight and be quiet and pray the plane is going in the right direction.

"You look very nice are you going somewhere for work or something?" she says kindly as she eyed my outfit.

"I'm on my way to New York City for an interview. I'm pretty nervous."

"If you do half as good as you look I'm sure you will nail it!" she says positively.

"Well thank you, I hope you're right. Enjoy the flight," I say.

I thought that would be the end of our conversation when I said, "Enjoy the flight" but instead, she started singing the itsy bitsy spider to her baby.

"Does the singing bother you? If it does I can stop, he might cry, but I don't want to be a nuisance," she says as she pulls out a pacifier.

I don't want to be a bitch so of course I tell her it's no problem. I'm being short with her so she will sense my perturbed demeanor as glib. What I really want to say was, "YES IT F'ING BOTHERS ME AND EVERYONE ELSE ON THIS PLANE!" as I sit and give her a demure look of unhappiness.

My heart starts to pound as the flight attendant announces we're about ninety miles out from JFK and making the initial descent into the city. I feel my palms getting sweaty which rarely happens unless I'm going into a nerve-wracking situation.

I know ninety miles is probably only about fifteen-twenty minutes away, so naturally I'm starting to have a minor anxiety attack. I'm annoyed at the lady next to me, but the baby finally fell asleep. She's really nice; I didn't mean to get so flustered, but this is literally the biggest day of my life. I just want some peace and quiet and time to think about what I was getting myself into.

As we are de-boarding the plane, she asks where my interview is, and I proceed to tell her Cosmo in the Hearst Tower with the address Human Resources gave in the email. She told me excitedly that she lives pretty close to that side of town. I'm smiling and trying to be nice when she blurts out, "Do you want to ride with us?" and of course, I'm thinking wow that's great and I really don't want to pay for a cab ride twice today. But this could be awkward. So without much thought, I quietly and shyly say, "Yes, that would be so nice."

I have time to kill anyways, and I don't have to be at the office until 1:30 if I'm being professionally prompt. I figure it would be nice to have a nice car to ride into the city instead of taking the train or a taxi. I wait with her and we finally get her luggage from the baggage claim area. At this point, I know her name is Lisa Quinlan. We walk to the parking lot, and she sets the alarm off on her car. I guess this is a safety tactic in case someone was following us.

"You need to know in this city it's dangerous for us women. Especially with a baby, you can never be too precautious," she said in a stern voice.

She was flying back from visiting her cousin, Annie in Florida. I don't know her address, but that's ok I figure she isn't going to kidnap me. Worst-case scenario I get sold into human trafficking. No big deal.

"Lisa, you seem like a really savvy lady. I think it's smart to be cautious. It's good for me to learn things like this since I might be moving here soon."

She's probably right about being overly cautious. I need to be aware of my surroundings because this is *not* the south anymore where everyone is your neighbor or friend.

I'm just trying to make amends for being a snob on the plane. Plus she's taking me, an absolute stranger, to the middle of the city and she really didn't have to. People talk about Southerners being nice...she is *really* nice for a *Yankee*.

Lisa has a nice midsize SUV; I think it's a Volvo or something European. I'm more concerned with my decision to get in the car with an absolute stranger who I wanted to slap sideways forty-five minutes prior. Her car does have a nice DVD player in the backseat that's playing a

Disney movie. Thankfully it helped put baby Ben to sleep. That's his name-Ben.

Lisa insisted I sit in the front seat so we could have a practice interview session. She said she'd ask me some questions to prepare me.

"So, Scarlett, where did you attend college?"

"College of Charleston," I said after I stuttered my response like a quivering idiot. I'm so nervous for my interview it's like I forgot everything about myself.

I really need to get my mind straight before this interview. I'm actually relieved Lisa is kind enough to ask me some questions. She's really smart. Before she had Ben she worked as a divorce lawyer for a big law firm and graduated from NYU. Her husband works for a private hedge fund here in the city. I can tell they have money because I know it costs a lot to have a car in the city. Lisa might be my guardian angel in disguise.

As we pass Macy's and all of the other big department stores like Bergdorf's and Bloomingdales, she tells me I should do some shopping while visiting. I tell her I'm flying back tonight, but hopefully, I'll be back soon. We exchange phone numbers and information as she pulls over to the curb. Lisa wishes me good luck and says she's so happy she met me. I feel somewhat relieved that she made my trip into the city so easy and accommodating. She kindly offered me a place to stay next time I visit; might have to take her up on that.

I notice quite a few restaurants around the building, and I'm starving by this point. I really want Shake Shack, but I decide on Au Bon Pain to grab a salad and soda with some caffeine to wake me up. I didn't want to eat too much before this interview because I tend to get squeamish before important meetings. The last major interview was in Los Angeles, and I got so sick before I walked in my face was white as a ghost. I ate a *huge* burrito with chips and guacamole at Chipotle before; looking back on that decision it wasn't my best. I'm trying not to relive that moment today. Needless to say, I'm glad that happened in that interview to prepare me for this one.

The time is passing swiftly; it was nearing one P.M., and I had thirty minutes to kill. I really don't know what to do or where I am to be exact. I had only been here once a few years back. I make my way to the Starbucks around the corner because I know they had free Wi-Fi. It's only a couple blocks away so my feet won't suffer too badly in these heels. I'm not sure if these heels are interview appropriate but when you're 5'6 you have to give yourself some power. High heels and standing tall can make a girl feel like she can conquer the world.

I decide to call my mom and check in with her to let her know I made it safe and told her about Lisa, the nice lady who took me under her wing. She saw I'm basically an NYC virgin and really helped me out. My mom told me to remember to think before I speak and to smile. I sometimes look too serious when I'm in an interview, and it comes off as miffed or scared. I have to come off as witty and charming. I think I can do that. I'll give them some Scarlett *Southern* charm.

Six

Concrete Jungle

I've never worked in a building quite this tall. I've been in them for touring purposes, but I've never actually *worked* in one. The elevator shows forty-six floors. Hearst Tower is literally in the middle of the city. Cosmopolitan Magazine is on the 26th floor, which is good because I might panic if I had to wait any longer on a crowded and smelly elevator. The entire building felt like a museum. It looks new, but I know nothing in NYC is "new." It was cold in the building too. Cold also meaning the décor is not very inviting when you walk in.

The elevator is crowded with men and women executives on their cell phones talking business and chatting to their significant others. I'm standing next to a lady who's dressed impeccably. I want to ask her where she shops, but that would be so lame. She had on a light tan suit with a white button-down and a layered gold necklace. Nude pumps just like me, but I'm sure hers are Christian Louboutins. Maybe if I land this job, I'll buy some of those 'red-bottomed' shoes.

Finally, I reach the 26th floor where my future awaits me. It looked bright and calming in the waiting room, much like a yoga studio or an upscale boutique. Dark cherry hardwood floors, expensive art hanging on all the walls, posters of the recent magazine covers. They even have water bottles next to the couch that has Hearst Magazine on the label. They are obviously neon pink with all the different popular magazines listed such as Marie Claire, Elle, and Cosmopolitan to name a few.

The receptionist isn't at her desk when I walk in so I just look around and wait anxiously. I sit down on the couch that probably costs more than my college degree. I see people walking down the hall. The offices have the privacy glass; the frosted kind you can't see through. I see a young woman walking towards the reception area, and I'm hoping she'll tell me that they're ready for me because it's now 1:59 and I'm getting antsy.

She told me that they were running a couple minutes behind with their other candidate, but they would be done shortly. Of course, I'm panicking in my mind because that means I have competition. I should have known I would in this type of position. They have to be thorough when picking someone to write for their magazine.

When I go to an appointment, I'm cognizant of time. I'm rarely *ever* late it's something I pride myself on. I'm VERY annoyed at this point because my flight is at 6:15 P.M. and it's now 2:15. I probably should've booked it for later. I didn't predict it taking very long. Then again I didn't really know what to expect they just told me when to be there and bring my resume. The receptionist finally took me to the room where they would conduct my interview. She took me to their big conference room with a huge oval marble table and expensive gray linen fabric chairs with armrests on each of them. My mom wanted these for our kitchen table, but my dad talked her out of them. So she bought some like this when they divorced. I sat there with my *fancy* water and silenced my phone. I said a little prayer in my head and hoped for the best.

A few moments passed and just as I finished reapplying my nude, light pink lip- gloss for the hundredth time, a woman walks in and introduces herself as Cabot, one of the Assistant Editors for Hearst Magazines. She looks pretty young to me. I would guess twenty-five or twenty-six judging by the engagement ring. She's really well dressed and friendly too. I'm not sure why I flew to NYC to interview with someone so young, though.

"I'm going to give you the writing portion of the interview. You'll have forty-five minutes to complete it. It will be a good judge of how you can write off the cuff in a short period of time," Cabot said in a very formal tone of voice as if she had done this several times.

I'm sitting here thinking, umm I did not prepare for any kind of writing test. They didn't warn me of this, and I didn't see it on any of the Glassdoor reviews I read online that I tried to prepare myself for this interview with. Luckily she gave me an AP Stylebook and a mechanical pencil. I'm starting to get worried about my flight again. It will take at least forty-five minutes to get to JFK…and I'll need to be early to check in. UGH! What a nightmare.

I start my test, and it's pretty easy, so I breeze through it and check my work a few times. I feel like this must be a joke because it is so easy. The test was mostly editing for errors and picking correct word choice in sentences. Then I had to edit a passage where I used correct writer's punctuation marks. I was finished in thirty-five minutes. I told Cabot I was finished. She took it from me and said that Nicole would be in shortly. I'm hoping shortly is less than ten minutes. Lucky for me it's five.

Finally the real part of the interview; the part where I can talk about myself and hopefully not mess up what I had practiced earlier before I walked in this place.

"Scarlett, nice to meet you finally; sorry that took so long. We don't like to tell our candidates about the test because it has stressed them out in the past and it worried them so much they did very poorly. I hope you did well because your resume puts you at the top of our list for candidates," said Nicole.

"Nice to meet you as well, Nicole. I'm very excited to be here, and the writing test was no problem. I really enjoy writing which is why I'm here today."

I'm starting to wonder when I would have to lie. I'm hoping I won't have to do so verbally.

"I see that you graduated top of your class at Columbia. That is very impressive. We have some employees in the office that graduated from Columbia maybe if you get the job you will see someone you know."

WTF! My face turns fifty shades of Scarlett. It turns out Addison DID indeed send that resume from our drunken night out. I can't *believe* her. I don't know what to do so I just *roll* with it. It's not likely they'll be happy if I explain the situation. Nicole would probably laugh in my face and tell me to have a nice day. I doubt they take kindly to rambling explanations.

"Well umm, my best friend sent that resume in and this is my real one. Please don't be mad. I'm really qualified!" Yeah right, I can't say that. I can't back out now; I'm ball's deep. I just smile and nod.

"Well let's move on to hearing more about yourself and why you think you could work for Hearst Magazines in our Cosmopolitan sector," she said in a very matter-of-factly way.

I give her the full run down about why I'm the perfect candidate and how I've dreamed of working for a company like this my entire life. Probably the mundane speech everyone pitches when they interview with her. This is the honest to goodness truth, though. I have to pull myself together and not worry about the mess Addison had created for me.

I tell her I like to write *fiction*, just thought it would be funny to throw that in there given my new circumstances. I want her to know I'm different. I try to convey I would be a *hard* worker. I'm a quick learn, and I get along well with everybody. I tell her I still have room for improvement as a writer because I want her to see me as humble. Nicole seemed impressed as she jotted some notes down on her tablet. Fancy way of taking notes if you ask me. I'm used to the interviewer using legal pads and writing directly on my resume with all their little-scribbled notes you try to read when they sit it down on the table.

"We're hoping to finish interviews this week. There probably won't be another round because we *really* need to hire by the beginning of October. You would just talk to someone over the phone, and we would make you the offer then if we decide to move forward. I hope that's ok with you," she said.

"Absolutely," I say with a smile from ear to ear trying not to look too suspect.

I couldn't be happier with the words that just came out of her mouth. I'm so relieved that I won't have to fly back in two days. I really can't afford another trip here. Then she said it would be a week before they called but they would call either way. She said I was a pleasure to meet with, and she is looking forward to working with me soon.

I shake Nicole's hand and make small talk. Nicole seems young and fresh-faced much like everyone else in this office. She said she lives in a building near mine. Apparently Claire lives in the building next to Nicole. Maybe that explains why Addison was *so* weird when I asked her about it; makes total sense now. She had already used the address on the resume she forged. I'm just trying to segue into new topics because I have absolutely no idea where Claire's apartment is but I'm glad it's apparently in a good neighborhood. I knew I would go home and start searching for places to live immediately and tell them once I'm hired that my lease was up, and I moved. Hopefully, that won't look too sketchy.

I walk out of that office feeling like a million bucks as cliché as that sounds. I'm so ecstatic; I can't even believe it's real. The interview didn't last long, but it was *good* while it lasted. I just hope I aced my writing portion. I don't second-guess myself much I have always tested well. It's funny how they don't mention the writing test prior to coming, but I guess that's how they weed out the weak ones.

I call my mom after I get in the taxi to head to JFK. I decide to leave early because it's already four and my flight leaves at six. Had I known the taxi driver was going to speed like he had a number three on the side of his car I would have taken my time walking out to the street. They don't ever warn you to wear your seatbelt but they really should.

Once I arrive, I grab a snack at the airport and FaceTime with Addison. I couldn't wait to hear her giggling through the phone. She's really excited for me, especially since she helped with the convoluted resume that landed me here. I guess I can't be too angry with her. I think I might have this job in the bag thanks to Addison applying for me.

After we hang up, I call my dad and he and Naomi were getting an early dinner, and he said he would call me. I'm glad I dodged that bullet. I don't like to talk to him when she's around. I feel like I'm doing my mom wrong when I divulge important things, and Naomi is privy before she is. I want to wait to tell my mom in person tonight when she picks me up from the airport.

I think it's time for some New York pizza and some cheesecake. I took my suit off in the disgusting airport bathroom and tried nicely folding it to fit it in my briefcase. Big enough to fit these stupid high heels in thankfully. I put my workout clothes on from this morning with my white low-top Converse, and I was a happy girl.

Now at my gate, I made direct eye contact with a guy I thought looked familiar. Of course, I'm trying to hide because I look terrible at this point with my hair in a topknot and these clothes from seven this morning. I look a little closer, and it looks like the guy I saw at Cosmo. Oh. My. God. He's coming near me. How could he be going to Charleston? Maybe he was going to Atlanta because that was my connecting airport. This is God's way of telling me that I can't get away with murder like I had planned.

"I'm not trying to be creepy or anything, but you look familiar. Do I know you from somewhere?" he said in the sexiest Australian accent I have ever heard. Nothing is hotter than an accent.

I immediately want to lie and just say, "No, of course not I just have one of those faces." But, instead, I say:

"I think you probably saw me interviewing at Hearst Magazines today."

Why didn't I just lie, I'm starting to become a great liar these days it would've been so easy for me. I'm literally in a tizzy right now trying to figure out what I'm going to say to him. I hope he doesn't call the office and say that I'm a fraud. I think I can distract him from asking too many questions if I casually flirt a little.

"Oh, that's right! I know a pretty face when I see one. I saw you leaving your interview with Nicole Ashley today. My name is Hugh Hamilton. I work in the photo department of Elle as a photographer." He said *oh so* charmingly.

He looks a good bit older than me. I love his look, though; it's *surfer* meets *chic* with his chiseled jaw and pearly whites. I love tall dark and handsome with light blue eyes. I'm trying to figure out what I'm going to tell him when I respond. Remember to think before you speak, Scarlett. Two ears, one mouth as my parents always reminded me growing up.

"I bet that's a really exciting job. When did you start working in the industry?" I said. I was curious about that because he didn't look to be my age.

"I started working for Harper's Bazaar in 2010 after I moved from Australia and started working for Elle about a year ago," he said with striking confidence.

I'm thinking to myself; he must be around twenty-eight or twenty-nine years old if he's been working that long. That's not that much older than me I guess. Wow, I'm already planning our wedding it's so typical of me after I meet a hot guy like this.

"So what are you doing at the airport," Hugh says when he casually clocks me up and down.

I just dropped the F-Bomb about fifty times in my head because I'm too caught up in his charm and good looks to come up with an appropriate response.

"Oh, I'm traveling home to see my grandparents in Charleston, South Carolina. It's my grandfather's seventy-fifth birthday this weekend," I spit out quickly.

It actually isn't a lie, and by miracle, I remembered that it's supposed to happen this weekend. I had forgotten until this very moment conveniently.

"You're from Charleston? I've only been a few times for work, but I would love to go back one day," said Hugh as he shuffled for his boarding passes.

I just want to tell him jump in my bag and come with me, but I try to stay calm and not act excited or curious at all.

"Where are you headed?" I say nonchalantly.

"Atlanta, Georgia for a short visit," he says with a very serious look on his face. Maybe he's just going there to work and not to see a girl. That's the silver lining I'm hoping for. My heart sunk though because that probably isn't the case. I've only known him for twenty-five minutes, but I'm totally lusting over him. Unfortunately, this is where I should probably stop asking him personal questions and move on completely.

Instead, I say this:

"Well, that sounds fun. In the event I do get the job, maybe I'll see you soon. If not, maybe I'll see you around the city sometime." I didn't want to ask for his blood type or social security number just yet. He's really nice, but it's awkward because I can't stop staring at his every move. I love hearing him talk I just want to sit there and have him read the Delta brochures and magazines to me over and over. I usually don't fall for a guy at first sight, but he's different than anyone I'd ever met. I feel like I could see myself with Hugh in the near future. Even if we're just friends; I can't imagine not seeing him again.

Seven

South of Broad

I'm sad we can't sit next to each other on the plane to Atlanta. My luck only happens when I don't need it to; plus I'm not sure what I would say to him. I don't want to tell him too much and give my true identity away. The good news is- I sat a few rows behind him so I can stare at him the entire way. It's really only his leg and the top of his head I can see, but I'm pretty thrilled nonetheless. I'm trying to think of how I could accidentally run into Hugh on the way to my next flight without it seeming like I'm trying to stalk him.

As we land, I decide I could maybe walk by him and pretend to drop something like my keys or a pack of gum. Then he could get a good look at my ass and come to Charleston with me! No, that's too desperate and obvious. I will just 'let it play out'.

I hear a sexy deep male voice behind me, and I'm so happy that it's Hugh. Now I don't have to figure out a way to stalk him.

"Scarlett, when do you think I'll see you in the office?" He said curiously.

"I hope very soon, Hugh," I say with a sultry smile while reaching for my next boarding pass.

We say our goodbyes and wave to each other as we went our separate ways. I really don't want this day to end. It has been so wonderful that I could jump in the air, click my ankles together and shout, "I LOVE MY LIFE" but I won't because the airport is no place for that noise.

I walk to my gate and board my flight. I'm not sure I've ever been this excited to go home. I can't wait to tell mom and Savannah the good news. The news being that my interview went well, not the news of meeting my future husband.

It's close to midnight now, and I arrived home. I'm starving at this point. Flying and walking around the airport always seems to work up my appetite. My mom offers to cook some breakfast when we get to the house, and I couldn't be happier. Thankfully it's Friday (technically Saturday but who considers midnight the next day, really?) so I will sleep in tomorrow and mom and Savvy would be there.

I tell my mom all the details I could on the way home and again while eating my mom's famous banana pancakes. She seems genuinely excited for me I can tell she's really proud of what I did today. She told me she would have got a hotel room for me, but she knew I'd want to be home for grandfather's birthday.

I went to my room and took a long hot shower. I feel disgusting and full of germs after being on a plane and traveling that long. I put my very comfortable terry cloth robe on and my hair in a soft, fluffy towel. I grab my Mac and immediately get on LinkedIn. I want to stalk Hugh on every social media outlet possible. I want to see his every detail. I sound like a real stalker, but I'm crushing so hard. Naturally, I find his Facebook page and see pictures of what I suspect to be his *girlfriend*. She's drop dead gorgeous. What could I expect? He's older and wiser so of course he's probably in a relationship. I'm a little *salty* as my sister likes to say. I wonder if Hugh looked me up on here as well. After stalking Hugh for roughly an hour, I'm exhausted and can't keep my eyes open any longer. I fall asleep after only a few minutes, and I slept so hard all night. I woke up late the next morning feeling happy and refreshed. I know I'll be on cloud nine for at least a week. New York City has such an amazing effect on me.

I start looking on Craigslist for apartments. I don't want to live with just anyone so I found a website that helps match you with the perfect roommate. I really wish I knew someone from school to live with, but then I would have to explain my *lie* to them. Maybe it's best just to meet someone that doesn't know me at all.

I really can't believe the prices of these tiny apartments with no washer or dryer, no dishwasher, and no air conditioning. I have no idea how I'll be able to afford living here.

I didn't ask the salary at the interview because I figure that will come once Nicole or HR calls me with the offer. I guess I can reevaluate then if I can even afford it. Maybe I will be asking for a loan from grandfather after all.

I spent most of the afternoon with my mom shopping on the island at some of the boutiques. We took a nice long walk across the Ravenel looking out at the Cooper River-my favorite activity. I told her about Hugh and how he is drop dead gorgeous. I told her about his age, and she didn't seem too worried about the age difference between us.

"I think it would be refreshing dating a man instead of a boy, someone who owns blocks, not plays with blocks," she said.

My mom would think that because she's dating an older man. When I say older, I'm only talking ten years older. Not *that* big of a difference obviously but it's different than what we're used to. He's a wealthy man who owns a marina here in Charleston. His name is Gray Stewart. I met him in the spring at the Charleston Cup where my mom introduced Savvy and me. He was polite, but he was clearly trying to impress us. We didn't think it would last long, but they have been dating nearly a year now. He doesn't come to our house. She usually just goes to his huge mansion on Sullivan's Island. I want to go to his house this summer and ride on his boat-without Gray that is. Don't get me wrong; I like Gray just fine. I just worry for her happiness. That's all that matters to me.

After going to the grocery store, mom and I decide to have a cookout for our little family. A *perfect* weekend so far. I couldn't get Hugh out of my head but other than that I'm doing just fine.

On Sunday, we went downtown to SOB (South of Broad) to my grandparent's historic antebellum home on the Battery. It's beautiful. Light pink, black, and white like Barbie's house. They have a huge wrap around porch on both floors of the house with white columns, said to help circulate the humid Charleston air in the summer time. It's an amazing place to live if you can afford it, but not many can. It's worth a lot more now than when they originally bought it. A lot of movies are filmed here. Meeting Street is pretty famous. He says it used to have charm and solace. I heard Gossip Girl filmed here a couple of years ago, but I never got to see it.

They have a carriage house in the back where my sister and I used to play with our dolls. My grandmother made it our playhouse until we got older and it became my residence my sophomore year of college until I graduated. Now it serves as a storage area for them I suppose. My grandparents bought a lot of land in Charleston when they got married in the 1940s. They owned so much property that the Riley name got very popular around town.

My mom was always in private school, and she grew up going to local charity events and galas. Not atypical for a wealthy child in the low country. My grandmother, Lucienda, or "Lucy" Riley as she goes by, was the head of the Debutant Society in Mt. Pleasant for nearly forty years. She always tried to get me to become a "Deb", but it wasn't my thing. Lucky for grandmother, Savannah is already excited to join.

My grandfather, Frank Riley is a Vietnam veteran, and he does a lot of work with the Wounded Warrior Project. He also works with Veterans on Deck here in town. This means he gives a lot of money each year to help veterans who come back from war and have PTSD to help them rehabilitate.

Kate, my mother, is an only child now. Her brother, Jack passed away when he was thirty-six in a bad car accident. It wasn't his fault. Uncle Jack went to the grocery store to get some cold medicine for his wife, my Aunt Liz. Some drunken guy hit him late at night and walked away without a scratch. The man is in jail now for life. My grandfather sometimes visits him to make him feel guilty. I think it's strange. But maybe it's because he was the last person to have interaction with Jack. We don't see Aunt Liz much because she moved to Seattle to start a new life. They didn't have kids, so she just packed up and left. The death of her husband changed her completely.

My grandfather is one of the best human's I know. He's exceptional.

I've always had a special connection with him. He helped me learn how to ride a bike, drive a car, and drive a boat. You have to have your boating license to live in *Chuck Town* according to him.

I think he looks pretty damn good to be seventy-five years old. I'm so happy he's healthy and still able to do fun things with me. Today we are taking their boat to get dinner at the Boat House on Sullivan's Island. It's a grossly overpriced restaurant but great ambiance and a great view of the water. They know Frank there really well. He's been going to the Boat House since he was thirty years old. You would think you'd get tired of a restaurant after going for that many years. He says it's not about the food anymore, just the memories and nostalgia. He says it's the best sunset in town too. He appreciates a sunset more than anyone I know, but I appreciate that he likes the little things in life.

I made him a cake last night after dinner. Carrot cake, because it's his favorite. He only eats *my* cake on his birthday. Not the store bought kind. He says it's his gift, and he doesn't need anything else. I always give him a little something, though. I donated fifty dollars to the veteran foundation, and he was so happy that he nearly cried when I told him.

"Honey, I couldn't love you anymore than I already do," he said as he hugged me.

I'll be absolutely devastated if something happens to that man; he's without a doubt a saint! For now, he's in great health and so is my grandmother. I'm so blessed to have them in my life. I hug him back, and we enjoy an indulgent seafood dinner and a wonderful *Frank Riley* sunset. These are the little moments when I will miss living in Charleston.

The sky is painted a beautiful red-orange color, and the weather is divine. I love how warm it stays here throughout the year. New York is going to be a huge slap in the face when it's freezing in October. I usually wear shorts all year unless it gets down to forty degrees. Talk about a reality check.

As we get on grandfather's boat and head back to the marina where he docks his boat, I try to take in as much as I can with the scenery and my family. I get chills every time I see the Ravenel Bridge over the Cooper River. I used to run the Cooper River Bridge Run when I was in high school with my parents and sister. When I got to college, I promised them I would continue, but I hurt my ankle the last time I did it. The truth is- I'm not in as good of shape as I was then and I didn't want to be lame and walk it. I told grandfather I would walk it this year with him. It's not lame if I do it for him. I'd do anything for him.

I'll miss that bridge, but soon the Brooklyn Bridge will amaze me just as this one does. I'm talking as if I'm moving and I got the job. I'm trying not to get ahead of myself, but the way Nicole talked to me in my interview seemed pretty positive. I will know soon enough.

Eight

Like Watching Paint Dry

The next few days felt like a year. Like most people, waiting to hear from a job is like watching paint dry, slow and *unbearable*. I need to do something to distract myself, so I'm going to help Addie pack for school. I need some girl time before she leaves in a few days. She lived in a house with three other girls from school, downtown. She had the best house for parties. I didn't want to live there because there is no way I could graduate on time had I done so.

"Hey, can you help me with this box? I need to get rid of some of these clothes before I move." Addison isn't one for heavy lifting.

"Are you giving me free reign to take some of these off your hands? I think that's the least you owe me for putting me in that God awful situation in New York," I say crossing my arms to prove my point.

"I know you're aggravated, but it doesn't even matter. You got the interview, and you'll probably get the job. You should be thanking me!"

I guess I can't be too mad at her. She's about to give me half her wardrobe so I can't be too upset.

Addison is constantly getting clothes and getting rid of clothes. Half of my wardrobe is Addison Webster's most recent Nordstrom catalog.

I'm totally fine wearing her old clothes. When I say *old* I mean a *year* old or less. She takes almost all her stuff to the dry cleaners, so she doesn't have to wash them. She'd take her panties if she could.

Addison isn't much of a neat freak. Her room looked like a tornado had flown in every time I stayed over. I used to come over before we'd go out and help her clean her room. Mostly so I could have a place to sleep that night. She spent a lot of time playing soccer for CofC. She got offered a full ride to play when she was a junior in high school. She traveled up and down the East Coast playing on a CASL team and got scouted at Duke University during a tournament.

"I want to hear all about this Hugh character after we're done boxing everything up," she said.

"There's so much to tell, and then again there isn't considering I don't really know him."

It's very possible I will never see him again. I don't want to think like that, though. I'm trying to stay positive. After packing Addison's things for law school, we decide to get our nails done. I don't have the money for frivolous activities but she does, however, it's probably the last time we can do this for a while. It sucks to think about our friendship dissolving after we go our separate ways. We have been linked at the hip for the past four years it seems. When she was a sophomore, she moved in with some of her teammates, and we didn't see each other as much as we did when we were roommates.

"Who are you going to hang out with when you move to New York City? Will you know anyone?" says Addison with a concerned look on her face.

"I don't know anyone except Lisa Quinlan, the lady I met on the plane who took me to the interview. There's Hugh, but I don't really know him yet, I just fantasize about knowing him. I do know a couple of girls who went to NYC for internships. I should see if they got jobs there after school."

The truth is I don't know them that well. According to the resume *I* created we were in the same sorority. Not the one *Addison* created. I'll have to look them up on LinkedIn later tonight when I do more apartment investigating.

"Well, you know my sister Claire and her roommate would probably be glad to show you the lay of the land. I'm planning on going there for my Spring Break if I don't get an internship."

"That would be really nice. I don't even know Claire I've never met her."

"Claire would love you since I do. I'm sure I could make a phone call and introduce you in an informal way. She's easy to be around-just like me!"

It would be nice if Claire would let me crash on her couch for a while. I know that NYC apartments are very small though and usually only has one bathroom. That would be such a nightmare trying to share a bathroom with two other girls in the morning getting ready for work. I believe that's about to be my reality whether I stay with Claire or live with random girls.

"I'm sure she's a great girl just like you, Addie. Thanks and I would love to spend some time with her and what's her roommate's name?

"His name is Perry Adams; he's from New Jersey I think," she confirmed.

Even though I've never heard a name like, Perry, I like it. My parents said that my dad got to name me, and my mom got to name my sister. My dad said that my cheeks were so red when I was born that they were nearly a shade of *Scarlett*. I thought it was kind of sweet. I watched *Gone With the Wind* and thought otherwise. My mom named my sister

Savannah after her favorite memory in Savannah, Georgia with my dad. They went there on their first trip to the South during their senior year at Pepperdine. She wasn't quite ready to take him home to her parents yet but wanted him to experience the Southern states. She was afraid they wouldn't see what she saw in him. I guess after the divorce she finally realized he might not have been the right one for her after all. My parents never regret marrying though because they have two beautiful daughters from it. They fell in love with the area and ended up living in Georiga when they got engaged. They got married six months after that and moved to Charleston.

After drying under the heat lamps at the nail salon, we look at each other trying to figure out our next move. Addison is one for planning. She always had an agenda.

"Do you think we should end this lovely afternoon with a pumpkin spice latte?" Addison pled like a child begging their parents for ice cream or a toy.

"Sure, but you know how I feel about paying *five* bucks for a drink that last all of *five* minutes. I'm sure I'll have to start drinking them in New York because you see people holding those cups all over the city like they are advertising for the place."

Addison spends close to eighty dollars a month on her Starbucks gold card. Her parents are what I consider wealthy and send her an allowance each month. I guess since they hardly ever see her she gets spoiled a little more. They rewarded her for her good grades where my parents just *expected* me to do well in school. I did well my senior semester, and my grandmother took me shopping on King Street. She told me I could "go crazy" if I wanted. She says it's fun to shop for clothes at my age but not at hers, so she just lives vicariously through me.

"I'm not really a coffee drinker, but I must admit that I'm fond of these fancy concoctions. Maybe I'll get a gold card one day like you '*Miss Thang*' I said to Addison in a very Cheshire kind of way.

"You'll need to learn to like caffeine when you're writing articles and staying up late with Hugh," she said sarcastically.

This is the last time I would see Addison before she left for school in a couple of days. We said our goodbyes and love you and whatever else best friends do before leaving each other for a long period of time. I'm going to miss her, but hopefully, she'll be able to visit in the spring.

The thought of doing anything with Hugh got my heart racing. I seriously feel like I did in middle school when I fell for a guy named Blake in my science class. I would get butterflies going into that class knowing he sat at the table to my left. He didn't know I liked him, but I was quite obsessed with him, in a *middle school kind of way.*

Hugh seems so sophisticated. He looks very put together with his nice big watch and his tight dark jeans. His hair spiked in the front ever so slightly, and he smelt so good even though I was standing at least a foot away from him. I don't think it was cologne, though, I think he just had that after shower smell. I *need* to know this guy. I desire to know more.

I'm going to be disappointed next time I see him if he blows me off because he's a *jackass* in reality. It doesn't seem like he could be that way from our first interaction. Men are hard for me to figure out. I'm probably going to end up getting a Tinder account and meet several creeps until I can find Mr. Right. I should start reading some of the columns in the magazines that give tips on how to date a guy or how to score the man of your dreams. For now, I'll hopefully just see him in my dreams.

Nine

The Call

I hear my phone ringing from my mom's bedroom, so I run in there as fast as I can so it won't go to voicemail. Lately, it's an appendage to my hip. To my surprise, it's a New York City area code, so I know it's probably the call I've been waiting for since I interviewed.

"Scarlett Hanes?"

"Yes, this is she!"

"Hi, this is Susan Williams the HR Director for Cosmopolitan Magazine. I'm calling you because the company would like to offer you the position if you're still interested."

Fireworks are going off in my head, and I don't even know how to respond to her. I'm silent for nearly twenty seconds when she asked if I'm still there.

"Yes, of course, I'm still here. I am so honored and excited and would love to accept the position!"

"That's great to hear, Scarlett. We're excited for you to join our team, and we look forward to you starting soon. Nicole said she would like you to start in two weeks. That's if you need to work a notice."

That's a relief because I still don't have a place to live, and I need time to get all of my crap in a pile and move up there.

"Yes, that is great for me. I can start in two weeks no problem. Nicole didn't mention salary or benefits when we interviewed. Could you give me some insight?"

"That's going to be the next thing I discuss. The company is offering you sixty-eight thousand a year with full health benefits and a discounted membership to a workout facility we send our employees. You'll receive three weeks paid vacation a year. We do give raises annually if we see the employee is doing an exceptional job- so just remember that. If you feel the need to counter the offer it could delay some things if not just let me know. I'll send it in an email, and you can fax it back to us as soon as you sign the paperwork," said Susan in a very professional way; almost as if she's rehearsed it.

"Susan, that is more than generous, and I will accept the offer. I look forward to receiving the documents. I will fax them as soon as I'm done signing them."

Susan and I ended our eighteen-minute phone call, and I started my Tuesday with the biggest smile on my face. I'm the happiest girl in the world. I feel like I conned them into selecting me, but I know I can prove myself. Sadly, my entire family thinks I will have earned this position on my own. Maybe they liked my personality or my writing samples.

Throughout the day, I couldn't stop thinking of all the amazing things that are about to happen in my life. The first thing that popped into my head was *Hugh*. I can't wait to see him again. I think regardless of us ending up together, we could be friends. It will be nice to feel like I know someone when I show up to a city I literally know no one. I need to call and cancel my car insurance because I won't be driving there.

There are so many things I need to do before I leave. I have to go shopping for an entire wardrobe. I might be able to ask my grandmother to take me since she enjoyed it so much this summer. Maybe she'll enjoy dropping another few thousand on my work attire.

We went to Shem Creek my favorite place to eat and look at the boats pass by on the water. My whole life is about to change. I can't believe I did it. I'm going to work at the magazine of my *dreams*. I feel like I'm actually living a fairytale. My parents were both so excited for me when I told them the news at dinner. Sometimes my mom and dad are civil and do things with their daughters. Savannah seems a little sad because she and I have become sort of close this summer despite how annoying running her around town has been.

"Sweetie, I knew you could do it. I've always believed in your abilities. We're going to miss you so much, but we can come visit. Have you figured out a place to live yet? I know rent up there can be quite pricey," said my dad in a loving manner.

"Yea, I'm still working on that part. I haven't figured out where to live, but I did meet a really nice lady on my flight, and she seemed eager to help me."

Maybe I should call Lisa. I'm sure she would be thrilled for me. It's possible she might even let me stay at her place for a few days until I figure something out. After dinner, we said our goodbyes, and I went home with my mom and sister. I had a few celebration cocktails at dinner, so I couldn't drive. I didn't realize how fast the day had gone by. I had been on the phone all day trying to get everything squared away. I'm really drained. I guess I can call Lisa in the morning.

"Hi, Lisa, it's Scarlett Hanes! Do you remember me from our flight and you taking me to my interview a couple of weeks ago?"

"Hi, there it's so good to hear from you! I wasn't sure that I would."

Lisa sounds really glad to hear from me. That makes the next part of this phone conversation a lot smoother for me since I don't like to ask things like this.

"Yea, I wasn't sure either but I ended up getting the job at Cosmo. I'm supposed to start in two weeks. I'm nervous, and I can't wait at the same time. Only problem-I haven't figured out my living situation yet. I was wondering if you could help me find a place in a good neighborhood."

There was sort of a long pause that made me feel awkward, but she told me she was feeding Ben, so she didn't mean to stop talking.

"Sorry about that, it's hard for me to multi-task sometimes. Scarlett, how would you feel about staying with Donald and me for a while? We have an extra room since the baby is still sleeping in the basinet in our room. We really wouldn't mind. I wouldn't even charge you if you wanted to stay for a month to get on your feet. You would just need to buy the food you want to eat."

I'm thinking to myself that this sounds way too good to be true. But what other option did I have right now? She doesn't seem like a mass murderer or a crazy person.

"Lisa, that's so kind! I couldn't!"

"You can and you will! We can pick you up from the airport when you arrive. What day will that be?"

"I haven't booked my flight yet, but I believe the beginning of

October around the 6th or sometime that week. Where do you live so I can tell my parents all about it?"

Lisa is so cheerful and easy to talk to.

"We live in Gramercy Park in a Brownstone. I'll text you our address so you can share it with them. I'm so excited about you coming to stay for a while."

"You have no idea how much of a life saver you are. You're constantly bailing me out. I hope I can be of some help to you and Donald. Maybe I can watch Ben on the weekends so you can go on a date."

"That sounds great, Scarlett. We really need to get out more. Since he was born five months ago, I haven't even had the chance to get my hair done. That will be wonderful."

My mom always tells me "nothing is free, Scarlett" and I'm starting to wonder what I've gotten myself into. After I spoke with Lisa, I call my mom. She thinks it's a wonderful idea. She said she'd use the software at the office to do a thorough background check on the Quinlan's. It seems to me that they live in a safe and beautiful neighborhood. I would assume they are wealthy if they can take me in rent-free.

I'm still going to need to search for a place because I don't want to live in Ben's baby nursery for very long. I don't think it will be a problem for a few weeks, though. I doubt I'll be going out much while living at the Quinlan's; I think that would be strange. I'm sure the magazine will need me to work on several projects to catch up. I hope I'm equipped to do this job because there's no going back now. I keep telling myself that the writing test must have gone well, or they wouldn't have hired me. Surely they wouldn't hire me just because they think I went to Columbia or was at the top of my class. My resume was just a formality. I can show Cosmo they hired the right girl.

Ten

Deep Fried Everything

The first week of October rolled around so fast that I didn't see it coming. Talk about a reality check. I'm moving to New York City in three days, and I haven't even packed yet. I tend to procrastinate doing arduous things in life and packing is number one on my list of favorite activities to put off until the last minute. There were so many things I had bought in preparation for the move, but I can only pack so much in two large suitcases and two carry-on items. I have so much laundry to do, and it seems like mom and Savannah chose right now of all times to hog the washer.

"Savannah! Please finish your laundry I have to do this now because I don't want to do it when I get to the Quinlan's!" I say it in a shouting manner hoping it would get the point across.

She shouts back that I'm not the only one who lives in this house. I'm starting to think moving won't be so hard after all. The bad part about moving into someone's house is that you're limited on what you can bring. My mom says when I'm ready to move into my own place she will drive up to the city with a U-Haul or something to help get my place accommodated properly.

I want to think I'm doing the right thing moving in with strangers. I've had several video chats over the past week and a half with Lisa and Donald so they could meet my mom and talk to her before I move in. Their background checks came back almost perfect minus the several speeding tickets Lisa had on her record. I don't expect anything less from a New York driver. Riding with them is scarier than any ride at a theme park. I'm glad I won't have to be driving in the city. I plan on getting my metro pass as soon as I can. I added the NYC metro app that gives all the fastest routes to basically anywhere in the city. I don't think Lisa lives very far from the office, so that will save time and money for a little while.

I kindly gave some of my old clothes that I probably won't need in the city to Savannah. She gets giddy when I give her anything, especially my clothes. I think she's getting worried about living at home alone (most of the time) and cooking her own meals. She's about to be sixteen in a few months and will be driving on her own. My parents already told her she could have my Jeep. Hopefully, it will be in one piece when I get home.

Later that night I try to buckle down, and finish packing. I have clothes I can wear for a couple of days so I don't mess anything up that I was bringing. My grandmother was kind enough to take me shopping for an entire work wardrobe. She told me it could be part of my *birthday* present. My birthday isn't until February, but she needed an excuse to gift me all of these beautiful clothes. I'm surprised that she allowed me to have the liberty to choose what I want. She is old fashion when it comes to showing *any* skin. I don't want to be provocative at work, but I don't want to look Amish either. Working at a magazine such as Cosmopolitan allows me to show a little creativity and hone my artistic side. That being said, I don't plan on getting any tattoos or weird piercings. That would send my grandmother to the grave.

I bought a mini steamer so that I could look polished for work on the days I couldn't get my dry cleaning. I'm starting to wonder how many hidden expenses like dry cleaning that I will have living in the city. Lisa and Donald have a washer and dryer unlike a lot of places in the city. They said I could use it whenever I needed; I don't want to be a freeloader, though. My mom's sending me with a gift because she says that all southerners need to arrive with a hostess gift. I don't have much room in my bags so she got me a sizable gift card to Whole Foods that I can give them. Everyone eats so she figured they would appreciate that. It should help alleviate some of their cost since I will be adding to their utility bill soon.

Tomorrow we are all going to my grandparents for dinner-when I say *all* that includes my dad. This should be very interesting. My grandparents haven't forgotten about my dad's infidelity, but they are trying to remember that he will always be our dad. I'll get to have one last southern cooked meal before it's ramen noodles and week old pizza. My grandmother makes the best-fried chicken and pecan pie you've ever tasted. She learned to cook from their "help" in the early '50s. It wasn't uncommon to have a maid or two back in the day. They treated her very well too. Her name is Willie Mae; she was pretty young when she started 'helping' them. She taught my grandmother how to cook all the southern dishes she learned to make at home growing up. Willie Mae was in their life for nearly twelve years until she married and had a baby. She still lives in Charleston on the other side of town, and they see her from time to time for a Sunday night meal.

My mom always gets anxious before seeing my dad like this. She has to plan her outfit out from head to toe and wants to look her very best. It's funny how she still cares about that kind of thing even though they are divorced now. She probably wouldn't care that much, but Naomi is gorgeous, I hate to admit that about someone I have total disdain for. My mom is real. She has not touched her skin with plastic surgery, and she looks really good for her age. She swears by yoga, plenty of water, and a lot of sleep.

She called us girls to sit on her bed as she picked her outfit for dinner. I realized at this very moment that I wouldn't be doing this for a long time. I'm trying to be on my best behavior knowing that it will be a lasting memory for us. It's sad to be away from my family for so long and knowing I won't have many people in the city I can count on at first. I hope that I can make friends quickly, but I know I will be really busy learning the lay of the land.

"Do you think I should wear this black sundress or this top with jeans? I don't want to look like I'm trying too hard, but I want to look a little sexy," said my mom in a weird and embarrassing way to us girls.

"I think you should wear what makes you feel pretty." I always believed in that notion.

"I agree with Scar," Savannah chimed.

She went with the dress because it's still warm enough outside to wear one. I checked the forecast for New York, and it said it would be a whopping fifty-five degrees for the high and forty-five degrees for the low. I feel like that is a normal winter temperature for Charleston. It's going to be strange wearing a coat in October. I will probably freeze for the first few months getting used to the arctic air. I will actually be able to run outside for once. I can hardly breathe here with the humidity so thick you can cut it with a knife.

We arrive downtown to the 'Riley Plantation' as my dad liked to call it behind my grandparent's back. I guess it is a rather large piece of property considering the location on Meeting Street. Almost all of the houses are pretty close together, and you can say hi to your neighbor without even leaving your porch. I always thought it strange to be so close and have to pay that much to have a house there. It's prestigious to live on the Battery. I can't tell you how many engagements I've seen from the second story porch-swing. My sister and I counted sixteen in one week while we stayed there while my parents were in Hawaii.

"Hey, kid! I'm so excited for you. I'm glad we are getting to do this before your big trip tomorrow. I still want to take you to the airport tomorrow afternoon if that's ok." My dad is always so cheery despite the rolled eyes he was about to receive all night.

I give my dad a big hug and say, "of course, dad! I wouldn't miss this for the world. Yes, I would love if you could take me. But just you if you can."

I had to remind my sweet father that I don't mind being with him as long as Naomi is out of the picture. He thinks she hung the moon, so it's hard for him to see why she disgusts my sister and me; she is wrong on all levels. I want to like her because it didn't seem like she was going to be out of his life anytime soon, but I just can't. I had hoped he would try to fix things with my mom, but that hasn't happened yet.

We all walk in and give hugs and kisses. My grandparents have a little Jack Russell named Murphy that greeted us at the door. He is starting to look old, but he still wags his tail and jumps in our laps when we sit down. He is the sweetest animal I've ever known. My parents wouldn't let us have a dog, so it's always fun to come over here and play with him. He used to let me ride my bike, and he'd run beside me; a very obedient dog that never ran away and hardly ever barked. He doesn't do much running now we think he is just tired from being close to ten years old now; in dog years that would be pretty old.

My grandmother has the dining room table set with all her autumnal decorations. She is the type who decorates the first of the month when there was any kind of holiday around the corner. She likes everything to be proper for this kind of meal. She has sweet tea pitchers on both ends of the table. My dad learned to like sweet tea after living in the south so long. He basically forced himself to like it since he knew he would be *forced* to drink it.

The entire dinner was fantastic from beginning to end. I feel like I might explode now from all the food, but I'm happy I got to enjoy one last feast. My grandfather gave me a pep talk about living in the city alone at my age. He tried to warn me of the men who would try to date me, and all the crime that happens in the city-he didn't realize he was scaring me. My dad happened to agree with him on this subject matter. Everyone has told me these kinds of things since I told them where I was moving. They act like I'm not aware of my life and how to act. I know it's an over protective thing to do. I appreciate their concern and take it as love.

My dad left because he has to go down to the station for work. He is working on a double homicide case that we weren't allowed to know anything about. My grandfather likes to smoke a cigar after dinner, so he went outside to do that as the girls sat in the living room to talk.

"Scarlett darling, your grandfather and I have decided to help alleviate some of your expenses. We know you won't get your first paycheck for a few weeks, and we don't want you starving. It should be enough for a month or so."

I look down at the check in awe. "What? Five- thousand dollars?! Y'all didn't have to do that. It's too much." I said shocked.

"Well I can make it a *lesser amount* if you'd like," she said in a cynical and funny way.

"No this is SO nice. I will pay you back as soon as I get my first check," I said with reluctance for her sarcastic statement prior to my response.

"Honey, we don't expect that. We have plenty of money and want to help you out. We helped your mom when she moved to Savannah with your father," she said in an annoyed tone most likely because that didn't pan out how she expected.

I didn't know they did that, but it doesn't surprise me. My dad didn't come from money, and they had just graduated and got engaged. Savannah seemed a bit sour that they were giving me so much money. She doesn't realize what it takes to be on your own. My parents pay for her every move. She'll understand really quickly when she gets to college in a few years.

I give my grandparents one last hug and thank them profusely. I don't know how I got so blessed to have them, but I'm never going to take them for granted-I do know that. It's so hard to leave them tonight because I know I won't see them until Christmas. I decided not to come home for Thanksgiving because it's only a few weeks away and only a few weeks apart from Christmas. I think my mom is planning on taking a trip up for a long weekend for Thanksgiving. We haven't missed Black Friday shopping in nearly ten years.

The drive home felt long. We sat in traffic for a while because the carriage ride tours were going on. This is the best time of year to travel to Charleston because it wasn't unbearably hot. We felt the tourism and traffic was certainly a factor of weather, wedding season, and it being a Friday night. The amount of October weddings we see here is incredible. Hopefully, I'll have one someday.

Eleven

The Last White Sailboat

Today's the day I change my entire life. My flight is leaving at six tonight, and I decided on a nonstop this time around. I didn't feel like agonizing over a delay or waiting a long layover. It was definitely more expensive going nonstop, but I'm so ready to be in the Big Apple. I have everything ready to go, and I'm dressed for the airport. I wore jeans and a flannel tied around my waist with a t-shirt because I figured it would be colder there. Of course, I'm going to burn up until then. It's nearly ninety today; record high for October.

My room is clean, and the bed is made. I decided to bring my pillow with me because I need some reminder of home. I have snacks packed in my bags and everything you need for a long trip. My mom is crying, and my sister is just glum. It's never easy to see your parent's cry, so that's why I had my dad take me this time. I knew it would be hard for my mom to drop me off today. She made me promise that I would call her as much as I could and video chat with her and Savannah. She taught my grandparents how to Skype so we could as well.

Leaving out of the driveway I too get a little nostalgic myself; I try to keep my cool, but suddenly I feel my face getting tight and really hot.

I'm trying so hard not to shed a tear but as I turn around my mom and sister were sitting in the rocking chairs on our front porch. I lose it. I think my dad feels bad for me because he knows I hate to cry. I seriously never cry, and I never do it in front of anyone.

"Scar, you're going to be just fine. I know it's hard to leave home and something you're familiar with, but you're a big girl. This is a huge opportunity for you to launch your career. I've always told you- the world is your oyster."

His words made me calm down a bit. I think it's perfectly normal for me to get emotional at a time like this. I don't like to wear my emotions on my sleeve like most girls. I try to be strong. I think growing up playing sports helped thicken my skin. I didn't have a brother to do the bullying, so I had to find my own way of coping with hard situations. My dad was my swim and soccer coach for twelve years. I thought I was going to swim in college, but I got sick my senior year and couldn't go to states. It was a huge disappointment considering I was hoping for that athletic scholarship. Thankfully I had really good grades in high school, so I did get half of my tuition paid for.

The days were getting shorter, I could tell. Usually, it stays really bright out until almost nine at night here in the summer. Daylight savings time is fast approaching and the time is flying by. I watch the sailboats pass by in the water and the ships off in the distance with all the containers on them. I've always wondered what it would be like to live on a ship like that. I don't think I would like that too much. I might not like living in a baby nursery either come to think of it. I do however love sailboats, but only the ones with white sails. There's something so beautiful about a sunset and sailboats on the water. I will miss looking over the Ravenel into the Cooper River at those boats.

"How long do you plan on living with these people? Have you even looked for an apartment?" he asked curiously as he focused on the cars in front of us.

"I'm not totally sure. They have a really nice place in Gramercy Park, which is a safe neighborhood. I'm trying to stay as long as I can handle the crying baby. I have looked at apartments, but they are either really small or in terrible locations. I'm hoping Lisa will help me find one."

We arrived at the airport around 4:45 P.M. since my flight was to take off at six this evening. It's hard to say goodbye to my dad, but I know he will probably come visit me soon. He has a lot of time off between his cases.

I went to check my bags, and one of my bags is over the weight limit. I didn't even care at this point I just want to pay the price and go to my gate. I should probably start caring soon because I think the money my grandparents gave me could burn a whole in my pocket really fast if I'm not careful.

The boarding area is really full. I guess these nonstop flights are rather popular. I might be able to get used to this. Hopefully, it won't be so crowded that they will have to bump me off my flight. That happened to my mom and me once when we were flying to a swim meet in North Carolina. My mom wasn't much for driving, so she flew us there, she can be sort of a diva at times. We ended up getting vouchers to use on our next trip, which was awesome because we flew for free for a few trips.

As I walk through the little tunnel going to get on the plane, I felt chills run down my entire body. I'm becoming very independent, and I like the new version of myself. I know this transition from home to the big working world will be difficult, but I wanted it really badly this summer when I was at home living with my mom and sister. I felt so depressed that I didn't have a "big girl job" yet and all my friends were already working at theirs. I have to remember times like that when I'm feeling down.

That felt like the quickest ninety minutes of my life. I can't believe the flight went by so quickly. It always seems like a long trip anytime you have a layover. This time was swift, and easy. I love it. I went to baggage claim and looked for Lisa and Donald. I looked for my bags, but they weren't there yet. I turn around and hear a familiar voice coming from the opposite direction. It's Lisa and Donald holding a sign that said, *"Welcome to NYC, Scarlett!!!!"* on this huge neon pink poster with bright sparkle letters. I can't believe they made me a sign. I think that is one of the sweetest things anyone has ever done for me.

I walk towards them and give Lisa a hug like she's my aunt or something familiar. I went to shake Donald's hand, and he pulled me in for a hug and said he doesn't do handshakes. I already sense the Southern hospitality from my new favorite Yankees. I have to realize that if I live in New York long enough, I will become one of those so-called *Yankees*. They're so excited to see me. Their next-door neighbor was at home babysitting little Ben. It's almost nine now, so I guess he would have been in bed hours ago.

Finally, my luggage came around the conveyer belt, and I went to grab them. Donald insisted on getting them for me since they looked heavy. He's friendly and made me feel welcome. Lisa and I talk about my flight and the free wine I got for sitting in the "economy comfort" seats. I told her I don't drink much, but she said that we could go for some cocktails next week to celebrate my first week of work. I think she was secretly excited to have a new friend to hang out with and do normal things besides breastfeeding and watching Sesame Street.

We walk to their car and talk about my life at home and my family. Lisa and Donald are already planning their trip to Charleston next summer for a visit. The weather here is already shocking my system. It feels balmy compared to how warm it was today when I left home. Luckily I packed a light jacket in my carry- on, so I was able to warm up with that.

They tell me they're excited to help me get ready for my first day of work on Monday. The ride into the city isn't bad this time of night minus all of the honking. It's cool for me to see all the bright lights and the Empire State Building lit up with its yellow and orange colors for the fall. I think it will be easy for me to fall in love with this city.

Twelve

Early Bird Gets the Bagel

We arrive at the Quinlan's three story brick Brownstone in Gramercy around ten after a forty-minute commute from the airport. They have several bright colored mums and haystacks placed on the stoop area of the entryway. There's also a decorative wreath on their door that had a big monogram on it, which made me feel even more at home. They don't seem to have front porch's here in the city, so that is something I'm going to have to get used to eventually. Donald opens the door to the house, and it smells wonderful- like lavender or something from a spa.

"Your home smells amazing. It's so beautiful here. I can't thank you enough for allowing me to stay."

I genuinely feel happy to be here. They are so kind and welcoming towards me.

"Thanks, Scarlett we are happy to have you here. I'll give you a tour of the home, but we have to be a little quiet since Ben is asleep," Lisa said in a whisper.

We walk down the narrow hallway to the kitchen and living room area. The Oriental rug leading the way is so gorgeous and regal. It reminds me of the ones in my grandparent's home, but it looks much newer. When we came in, we saw the babysitter. I expected someone really young maybe my age, but it was an elderly lady sitting in the chair watching television.

"Hi, Ruth, thank you for taking care of our baby boy while we were out. This is Scarlett Hanes." Lisa introduced in a polite way. "She will be staying with us for a while. She just moved here for her new job at Cosmopolitan Magazine."

"Hi Scarlett, nice to meet you, I live next-door if you ever need anything. Maybe you can get me a subscription to your magazine; I love reading them it makes me feel young again," said Ruth in a seductive way. It's kind of awkward the way she smiled when she said it.

"Thanks, Ruth. I'll be sure to ask if I can get friends free subscriptions. If not, I'll try to bring some from the office for you."

After Ruth left, Lisa showed me where everything is. I really just want to know where the shower is so I can get clean and go to bed. I'm so exhausted from all the emotions and everything leading up to this very moment. Not to mention I'm feeling a bit queasy from the anxiety.

The living room has brown distressed leather sofas and a nice big cream-colored loveseat. There are more Oriental rugs in the living room and kitchen area. They have a huge flat screen TV mounted on the wall above their fireplace that is currently burning. The house looks like something you see in a Pottery Barn catalog. The kitchen is fit for a chef with black sparkly granite countertops and white cabinets; a very clean and classic look. They have a huge refrigerator that looked like it was built into the wall and a white farmhouse sink that I'm in love with.

"You're welcome to anything in the fridge or pantry. I wasn't sure what you like for breakfast, but we were planning on taking you to this little deli around the corner for a bagel tomorrow. You have to experience it on a Sunday morning because they are so fresh and amazing," said Lisa in such an endearing way.

I thank her and give her the Whole Foods gift card my mom bought for them. They were both so sweet about it and tried to tell me to keep it because I would be buying my groceries. They said I could keep it and help them with their grocery list, and I could get what I wanted with it. I'm starting to wonder if they think I'm going to be their "free" babysitter and errand boy. I guess that's the price to pay for living at someone's amazing house without paying any rent.

After showing me the first floor, they take me upstairs. I'm trying to be as quiet as I can, but the floor is hardwood, so you hear things a little louder than you would on carpet. They have three bedrooms upstairs-the master where the baby is sleeping right now with a loud sound machine to block out the noise, the nursery where I will be staying temporarily, and a guest room that serves as an office and man cave for Donald. I have my own bathroom within the nursery, so that is really great. They don't have a crib in the nursery yet because they knew they'd want Ben in their room for at least five to eight months. They have a nice full-size bed up against the wall for me. It isn't huge, but it is just enough for me. The bedding looked expensive. I'm sure it's Egyptian cotton or something I've never experienced in my twenty-two years on Earth.

"We know you're probably exhausted, so feel free to go to sleep if you need to. I put some fresh linen's on the counter in the bathroom for you to shower if you'd like," said Lisa while folding some of Ben's laundry.

Donald went to bed, so I'm just talking with Lisa for a few minutes as I unpack a couple of things. Lisa, being that she's very kind helped me put some things in the closet. She created a space for all my clothes. Ben has a ton of really nice looking baby clothes, but they don't seem to take up much room. I feel like they've created such a warm environment for me as if I'm staying long term. She finally left my room, and I'm able to shower and get ready for bed.

The room isn't your typical baby nursery decorated light blue or light pink. She has everything white and gray from the bedding to the art on the wall. There's a nice gray glider that I could find myself missing when I'm gone as well. In the shower, the showerhead is incredible and huge; the kind with amazing water pressure without a doubt. The subway tiles are so modern, and the pale blue accents added a calming effect. It has a big bathtub with a beautiful white lilac shower curtain with Lisa and Donald's wedding monogram on it. The sink area is white and gray marble, which is fitting considering everything in the room, is white and gray down to the hangers in the closet. There weren't many hints of a baby nearby, but I'm sure once he moves into this room they will add some stuffed animals and toys to let everyone know its Ben's room.

I was right about the sheets feeling like butter. The white cotton silky sheets feel like something you would have at a luxury hotel. The silk gray linen duvet on top with pillows to match and I'm sure it wasn't cheap. I'm still trying to figure out how I got so lucky with this situation. Nothing seems to be wrong just *yet.*

It's now midnight, and I decide to send my parents and email telling them all about my adventure today. I want them to be on the email together, so nobody feels left out. I plug my phone in because it is about to die and realize there is a Bible in the drawer of the night- stand. I wonder if they go to church or if they just have that there because it's the thing to do in a nursery. I'm curious if they will want to go to church tomorrow morning. I guess they would have mentioned that in the car ride here so I would be prepared.

I slept like a rock last night-until five this morning when Ben started to cry: *loudly.* I totally forgot this could happen since there's an infant in the room across the hall from me. This could be the demise in this living situation. As soon as he stopped crying, I hear a slight knock on my door. I'm of course still lying in bed trying to fall back asleep at this point.

"I am *so* sorry Scarlett; I totally failed to mention that Ben is an early riser. I come in here to breastfeed him and let Donald sleep a little longer. I hope that won't bother you or make you feel uncomfortable."

Why no Lisa, you having your breast hanging out in the room while I try to sleep is no problem. In fact, why don't you turn the light on so I can get a better look!

"It's no problem Lisa. I'm the one invading your space. Do what you have to do." I said it quickly and quietly hoping she would let me keep sleeping.

"So how did you sleep last night? I hope you were comfortable. We just got that bed when we found out we were pregnant with Ben. We didn't think we would use it so soon. It's been in our basement for a while."

"I slept great, thank you again for having me."

Until now-I'm thinking in my head annoyed. It took her nearly fifteen long minutes to feed Ben and to leave me in peace. Luckily I'm able to fall back asleep. This is way too early for me, and I don't plan on waking up this early on the weekends. I don't want to overstep my boundaries by asking her to feed him in the office. It sure would be nice, though. I don't think I'm at liberty to ask those kinds of things yet. They've been so generous already I would hate to mess up their routine on top of it. I guess this is something I will just learn to live with for a short period of time. It's only temporary. I need to wake up early for work anyways.

Thirteen

"The more I see the less I know"

I was only able to sleep for another two hours before Ben needed to be fed again. This time, she did it downstairs, but thankfully everyone was awake by now. I guess this early is considered a normal hour in this household. Like I said, I need to learn to wake up early for work because it's going to be a rude awakening pun intended, come Monday morning when I'm stressed and nervous getting ready to be there by eight thirty sharp.

Today the Quinlan's are taking me to their favorite bagel shop, "Ess A Bagel" for breakfast and a tour around the city. We had to be back by two this afternoon for Ben's nap. They want to show me where the metro station near their house is because I'm going to be taking it into work tomorrow. They would take me on the route I needed to go as well. This is going to be really helpful considering I will be a bit frazzled tomorrow. I got an email from Cabot Vanderbilt, the girl who babysat me while I took my writing test. She informed me what time I needed to be in tomorrow and where I would be going. There was another list of things on the email that gives instructions about my lunch break and telephone usage while I'm working. She said she would go over everything with me in person.

We took the Volvo for our tour of the city so that we wouldn't have to walk all day. They didn't want me to wear myself out before my first day of

"School;" I mean *work*. It really did feel like the first day of school- all the preparation for such a new adventure. The baby's car seat sat next to me in the backseat. He's adorable I must admit, and really well behaved except when he cries at five in the morning.

The bagel shop is exactly how they described it to me. Something you see on the Food Network on one of their shows when they talk about the best thing they ever ate. This bagel might be one of the best things I've ever tried in my entire life. If I'm not careful, I will gain a lot of weight eating all the delicious food here. This is a concern to me because I'm somewhat of a foodie.

After breakfast, we venture off to Times Square. I haven't seen that many people in one place since the last time I was here. It's so surreal being that this is now my home. I can now say I live in New York City, and I'm not even lying about it. It feels good to have some truth to my story now. I hadn't even had much time to think about what I'll do or say if I run into Mr. Hamilton tomorrow at work. I've been so busy and preoccupied I'm not even thinking about him.

"Have you ever been to Bloomingdale's?" Lisa asked in an excited voice.

I could tell it was probably her favorite place to shop. Donald rolled his eyes as if he sees that on his credit card statement every month with a lot of zeros after the numbers.

"I actually have not been there yet. It was the one place we didn't have time to go the last time I was here."

The truth is, I knew I couldn't afford to shop there, so I just skipped it all together last time. I spent most of my time at the landmarks and art museums. Though I am interested in shopping there just to see what everything cost. It can't hurt to see what they have.

"We can go there for a little while and then we can get lunch before we head home. There's a really charming place to eat just outside the store."

Lisa and Donald are thin in my opinion considering how much they seem to eat. They look like they stay active somehow; maybe they have a home gym in their basement, which I haven't seen yet. Lisa is tall and has olive skin and short dark brown hair that almost looks black, and it's really shiny. She has bright green eyes that look greener depending on what she's wearing. She looks to be in her early thirties, but I haven't asked. I've learned not to ask anyone's age because it makes me feel really bad when I guess him or her to be older than they actually are.

Donald is pretty tall too and has salt and pepper hair like *McDreamy* from Grey's Anatomy. It looks like he's starting to age a little according to his hair color. He has light brown eyes and a scruffy beard. I'm sure he has to shave every day for work, so he lets it go on the weekends. I don't know anyone in finance that doesn't have that perfectly manicured look. He dresses nice too- I think he's wearing *Vineyard Vines* and nice brown leather loafers. Lisa is wearing black jeans and a *Burberry* poncho that looks like it's probably cashmere and dry clean only. Here I am wearing jeans with holes in the knees, a baggy sweater from *H&M* and my Converse. I fit in here in the city, but I don't dress as nice as they do. I save my good clothes for work, and they will see that tomorrow.

We made it to the shops on Fifth Avenue and went to Lisa's favorite place, Bloomingdales. They have plenty of security guards in nice suits watching your every move like they are spies on a James Bond movie. We went to a restaurant around the corner for lunch after looking at all the expensive watches I'll never be able to afford. It wasn't even noon yet, but it felt like it was much later since I woke up so early today. I'm not used to getting my day started and having a lot accomplished by noon. I guess I will be going to bed early tonight.

"This is one of the first restaurants we went to when we met ten years ago. We were probably your age then. Donald and I have been married for six years. We wanted to wait to have kids so we could live the life we wanted first."

I can tell she's happy with her husband; she has a genuine smile when she talks about their marriage and their baby. That means she is probably about the age I guessed. That is a good age to settle down and have kids in my opinion. I will hopefully wait longer than my mother did. She had me when she was twenty-two years old. I think that is way too young. That is probably why she had my sister seven years later. She wanted to wait until she was actually ready to have a baby. I guess I was somewhat of an accident if you had to guess.

"I'm really glad you have shown me so much today. I feel comfortable with you guys showing me around it seems like you really know this city inside and out."

I forgot that I'm supposed to contact Claire about showing me around. I will have to send her a message tonight before I go to sleep.

Lunch was delicious and thankfully they paid because every single item on the menu was close to twenty-five dollars or more. I didn't know they were going to pay so I just had soup and salad. That could be why they offered to pay because I didn't over order. I was still full from my bacon egg and cheese and large iced coffee this morning. I can't imagine what we will be doing for dinner if the first two meals were like this.

"I'm going to drop you and Donald near the metro station that you'll be taking into work every day while you're staying with us. I need to get

Ben down for his nap and Donald knows his way around the subway better than I do," Lisa said in a commanding tone.

I'm sitting here thinking wow that is a little awkward; leaving me with your husband whom I barely know at all to take me underground where there is no cell reception. *Sure* no problem!

"Sounds great, thanks for lunch see you soon," I said as we hopped out of the SUV onto the curb.

I say it with zero hesitations. I don't want her to know how I really feel about her *granny dumping* me with Donald.

"Don't worry, *love* I don't bite. I'm excited to show you around and go on your first subway ride."

Donald does seem nice, but it is a little weird how he looks at me. He doesn't look at me the way my dad or grandfather does. I'm going to try and not over think the situation and just take it for what it was-him showing me how to get my metro pass and how to get around in this huge city I now call home.

Lisa just placed me in a terrible predicament. I'm in a foreign city with a foreign man; a lot could happen. I have a very hard time trusting people, or should I say, men, that I just meet. Whenever I get nervous like this, I try to sing that Michael Franti *Say Hey* song in my mind to ease the anxiety. Something about a cheery song like that grounds me in a situation like this. Repeatedly singing the chorus in my head distracts me from the creepiness of this situation.

As we walk along the *filthy* sidewalk with Donald on the outside and me on the inside, I try to figure out just how I got myself to this very moment. I went out drinking with Addie; I faked my resume, I got an interview, I met Lisa on the plane, then I got the job offer, and moved in with Lisa and her wealthy husband in a very nice home. Sounds about right I suppose.

"Here's your station," as he points to the metro sign and walks across the crosswalk.

"Ok cool, I'm guessing we're about to get on a train to practice riding into work?"

I'm trying to play cool like I'm not freaked out being with an older, attractive man.

"You got it, kid."

It's kind of weird that he called me *kid* just the way my dad did in such an endearing way. Maybe he isn't hitting on me at all. Maybe he is just nice. My parent's divorce has totally ruined the way I perceive men. Someday I will learn to trust them but until then I will keep my guard up with an imaginary metal shield.

We went down the steep and disgusting steps filled with old gum and trash scattered everywhere. The amount of litter is just outstanding to me. This entire process seems really daunting, but I have to figure it out whether I want to or not because I'm certainly not walking into work tomorrow. As we get to where we need to be, I notice all of the homeless people sitting against the walls and the men playing their instruments hoping for spare change. I give one of the guys a dollar and Donald tells me not to do that. He says that they will expect you to do it every time, and they *will* remember.

We finally see our train speed through the tunnel to our stop and wait with the many people around us that were in a hurry to get somewhere. Everyone in the city seems to be pressed for time, or maybe they just move at a faster pace than we do in the South. Most everyone here is very thin, so it seems. Everyone is dressed differently, but weirdly enough they looked the same. I noticed that I'm going to need to invest in some headphones because nobody likes to talk on the subway apparently.

As we wait for everyone to clear the entryway so we can get on, Donald grabs my hand and pulls me close so he can shove me on the train as it is about to leave without me even noticing.

"Wow! They don't give you much time at all to get on these trains!"

I'm seriously appalled at the speed of these things. In the past trips I've been on, I never rode the subway. My parents didn't mind spending the extra money to taxi around because we weren't there long enough to waste time underground figuring our way around.

"Yea, these trains will come and go if you aren't careful. Sorry I grabbed you like that, but I figured you weren't expecting it all to happen so quickly," he says in a concerned voice with his eyebrows raised up.

I look around trying to figure everyone out as we wait to get to the next station. It is impressive to me all the elderly carrying their grocery bags around like it's no big deal. I can't imagine my grandparents navigating the metro stations alone. There are moms with their babies and young teenagers with their friends who looked up to *no* good. The range of ages on here is the most intriguing thing to me.

"Here's our stop," Donald says as he stands up while the train is still moving.

We get off, and everyone shuffles their way through the station to their next destination. We feel like we have to go fast because everyone else seems to be in a hurry. I follow Donald to the staircase on the right going towards Broadway. This is where the stop is to get to my office. When we get off, I feel like I have been on a ride at Disney or something; seeing the huge skyscrapers and all the people feel so surreal. The air smells like the pretzels you get at a baseball game, and the smoke smelled somewhat like the fair. A smell I could certainly get used to.

We walk a few blocks up and there it was; the building that held my future by forty-six stories of offices and working executives; the building that would change my life for the better. I can't believe this is where I work. I smile from ear to ear and finally have a sense of ease that I had hoped to feel like I do when I'm at home in *my* city.

The subway home was only eight minutes away making the trip feel swift and easy. It's an incredibly close journey that I could probably walk if I had to. Once the weather gets cold, I won't be able to withstand the temperatures in high heels. I figure taking the subway isn't so bad.

We finally make it back to the brownstone. I'm feeling relieved to know I won't have a terribly hard time getting to work tomorrow if I can manage not getting lost along the way.

Now I'm singing the song in my head because I'm *happy*, not afraid.

Fourteen

Hugh Don't Say…

I'm awake extra early today, not only because Ben was crying at three, four, and five this morning, but also because I want to look put together for my first day of work at my amazing new job. I curl my hair and put on a little more makeup than I normally do. Not only am I trying to impress my boss and my coworkers, but also, I know there is a chance I could run into Hugh. I decide on a multi-colored sheath dress with a black blazer and a long necklace as the accent piece. I pick my favorite nude round toe pumps and Dolce & Gabbana *Light Blue* perfume to spray on each of my forearms.

I don't have time for breakfast, so I plan on eating an apple at my desk or something to hold me over until lunch. I practically run downstairs, and Lisa has so kindly made me a smoothie in a to-go cup. I can't believe how thoughtful it was for her to prepare me something for my first day. I know it's something my mom would do. I thanked her and ran out the door with my purse and my briefcase.

I retrace my steps to the metro station and find my way down to the right terminal. I use the metro pass that Donald helped me get yesterday on our little tour of the underground world.

I got on and off the right train-I can't believe how easy it is to get around here in this crazy city. I did have to stand up the entire way, but I don't care. The adrenaline pumping through my veins today is at an all-time high. This is most definitely a fight or flight type of situation. It's emotionally taxing trying to adjust to a new city and start a new career if you're wondering. I have to be into the office early today to get shown to my desk and go on a tour of the office. When I interviewed, they didn't show me much because they probably didn't want to lead me to believe I had the job. I'm so excited to see what a big magazine conglomerate will have for their employees and all the added perks.

I walked in the doors of the Hearst Magazine office and was greeted kindly by the same receptionist from my interview last month. She made me feel extremely welcome. It's been my ongoing fear that someone was going to take this job away from me right as I start loving it. I still have that feeling in the back of my mind, but I try to put it aside and be excited and proud of myself instead for getting to this point.

She takes me to the break room in the middle of the office that all the syndicates share. There is a small kitchen area with a refrigerator and a Nespresso machine for all of the employees to utilize. The fridge is full of the same fancy waters from the lobby, diet sodas, and what looks to be craft beers. There is a basket full of snacks that we were allowed to take at any time during the day. She showed me to the Cosmopolitan sector of the office, and it had its own separate sitting area and office space in the back. It's decorated impeccably just as I had suspected. We walk around, and she introduces me to a few editors that I will be working with from time to time.

Then she shows me *my desk*; *my very own desk* with my *very brand new* Mac desktop and *very expensive printer* right next to it. My chair is a hot pink swivel chair, and I *love* it. There is a penholder with pastel colored sharpies and other writing utensils. I was under the impression that I would have to provide everything for my desk, but I forget the company I work for. This is Cosmo-one of the bestselling magazines in the world. The receptionist left me at my desk to get acquainted, and Cabot came by to say hello and wish my luck on my first day. She told me that they would probably assign me to write a segment even though it was only day 1. She said they were tough around here, and they babysit you. She was right.

"Hello Scarlett, my name is Courtney Hastings, I will be your Editor in Chief for the fashion segment here at Cosmo," she said while holding her Cosmopolitan coffee mug and her smartphone.

She gives me a couple of glib looks before her next sip. I have a feeling she is going to be difficult. This meant she is going to be my boss. I know I have to be on my best behavior around her and hope that she doesn't figure me out. The less I say is probably for the best.

"Hi, nice to meet you, Ms. Hastings, I'm excited to be here and ready to get to work."

"Please call me Courtney, my mother-in-law is Mrs. Hastings."

Seems like she is trying to break the ice, which is comforting. She isn't very friendly, though. I'm hoping she won't be the *devil wearing Prada* type.

Cabot wasn't wrong about the first-day assignment. Courtney told me that I am to write a short piece for the new "Fall Favorites" jewelry line by Thursday at noon. I wasn't quite expecting this so soon, but luckily for this particular piece I won't be writing a ton. I will just have to meet with one of the in-house designers and interview someone from one of the jewelry lines we decide on to figure out which pieces they want to use and get a quote from the designer. I think this will be a fun first piece to do. It will feel amazing to have *my* name next to it.

I can't believe how fast the day was flying by. It's already ten, and I have been at my desk researching the jewelry line I thought we should use for the segment. I met with the in-house designer, Cooper, and we decide on a jewelry designer to meet with and interview for our piece.

The only thing that will get me through this morning is a jolt of caffeine, so I went to the break room that everyone shares. I didn't expect to run into Hugh, but there he was pouring French vanilla creamer into his Vogue coffee mug. I wish I had looked at myself in the mirror before coming over here, but I didn't expect to see him in the first three hours of my first day.

"Scarlett, good morning, this must be your first day on the job? How do you like it so far?"

I don't even hear what he said because I was in awe of how drop dead sexy he looks in his work attire. He isn't wearing a suit, but he looks *really* expensive and chic with dark jeans and a black V-neck shirt and fancy sneakers I have never heard of called Supras. His hair is slicked back in a way I hadn't seen in any of his pictures-but I loved it.

"Good morning to you too, it is my first day, and it is going really well so far. How are you? Where is the Elle office?" I say hoping I was correctly responding to his question.

"We are actually adjacent to one another so we could be bumping into one another like this more often. I come in around this time every day for a coffee break and to catch up on my phone," he said with his super attractive accent that I had missed hearing so much.

Nothing sounded wrong coming out of his mouth. I try not to linger too long, or he will think I'm seriously into him-which I am. We say bye to each other, and I sadly go back to my desk. It's extremely hard for me to focus because all I can wonder is if I will run into him every day and have to think of him without clothes on. Just kidding!!!

I sit down at my little four-by-four cubicle and look at my surroundings. Everyone has very glossy and polished looking cubicles. I will have to invest a little money and procure some fancy items for my desk-décor. All of the other editors were chirping away on their keyboards, and I'm just off in *la-la land* thinking about interior design and a man I can't have. I'm notorious for getting off track. I blame it on my overly *creative* mind.

I get on the phone and set up an interview with a girl named Julie from the jewelry line that I would meet tomorrow at two in our conference room. I can't believe how much they are letting me have reign over so soon. It's formidable and exhilarating at the same time. I'm incredibly happy that nobody is sitting next to me or looking over my shoulder telling me how to do things I already know how to do. Having this kind of liberty makes me think it will be hard but also very maturing for me knowing I can accomplish so much.

The clock finally struck five, and I was gathering my things like everyone else in my section of the office. You would have thought Courtney fired an air horn and told everyone to get the hell out of here. I'm sure she is subliminally telling us that. I organized my desk the way I like it and thought I can add a few *Scarlett* touches to feather the nest by next week. I say goodbye to a couple of coworkers that I met earlier and got on the elevator with all the other executives.

I realize that I hadn't stopped to eat lunch today, so I'm starving at this point. The entire elevator might hear a loud roar in a second due to me being famished. I text Lisa to let her know I'm grabbing some dinner on the way home, and I'd be back later. I feel like I'm answering to my mom, and because this isn't going to work for me at all. I'm ready to find my own place and only have to answer to *myself*.

After grabbing some fast food and going to the drug store to get a few things, I take the metro to the Quinlan's and hope I could take a shower and wind down. I want to rest my feet up and watch some TV if I can. I walked in and told them I'm back and run upstairs to shower quickly and change into clothes suitable for chilling out. I didn't ask them permission to do things because I figure it would make things awkward.

It feels wonderful to take my heels off and feel clean after being in that disgusting subway station. My ebullience will be obvious to Lisa and Donald now that I'm relaxed in their very clean environment of a home. It's a surprise to me how one place can be so filthy, and nobody does anything about it.

The fire is burning, and the TV is on. Lisa and Donald are cuddled up on the couch close to one another, and they ask me to join them. I sat in the love seat and enjoyed the HGTV show they were watching and told them about my first day. There was something nice about coming into my new little family so to say. Regardless of answering to them, I still enjoy their company. They seem really interested in hearing all the details, and that's when Lisa got up to say goodnight and left me with Donald yet again. It's starting to become a trend of hers. Maybe she doesn't care that he is with me alone. Maybe they are in an open marriage or something. Maybe Lisa got off on Donald hitting on other women, and they made a thing of it in the bedroom-who knows. I can't figure it out, but I try to look busy scrolling through Twitter on my iPad so he won't make small talk with me.

It's almost ten P.M., so I decide to call it a night and go to my room and get ready for the next day. Donald gets up and grabs me a bottle of water from the fridge and tells me sweet dreams in a loving manner as he grasped my shoulder. I try not to over think it, but it still wigged me out considering he didn't do the same for Lisa. I went upstairs and picked my outfit for day two and hope it will go as smoothly as the first day. I text my mom to tell her about my day and couldn't believe how I missed being home. I'm going to have to distance myself in order to make it through these next few weeks until she comes for the holidays.

Fifteen

Zen there was Chase

This morning is flying by, and I knew I had a deadline to meet by, Thursday. I wish I could make time slow down a bit, but I have no choice but to get things done, or Courtney will throw my ass out. I'm meeting with the girl from the jewelry line after lunch today. I think I will actually try and leave my desk for lunch if I can get everything done before noon. I decide not to go to the break room in fear of running into Hugh again. I'm not ready to figure him out just yet. Not until this deadline is met.

I meet with Cooper again, and we pick the rest of the pieces for the segment. The only things I have to do are meet the girl, get a few quotes, and write the rest of the segment. I know I can pull this off because I'm a girl with determination. I have to be rational and remember I can't just throw this together. It has to be planned out accordingly and appropriately, so they are impressed with my first piece. I also don't want them to regret hiring me and wonder how someone from "*Columbiaaa*" could fall so short, *so* fast.

I save all my work to my desktop and grab my purse for lunch. I locked my briefcase in my bottom drawer and neatened my work area in case *Sergeant* Courtney is checking rounds. I get to the elevator and realize I have not idea where to go. There are so many dining choices in the city, and I didn't feel like an hour is long enough to figure out today.

I get on the elevator and press the button for the lobby of the Hearst Tower. A guy to my left is also going as he confirmed that the lobby is his destination too. He looks attractive with his dark brown hair and tan skin as I try to stare without him noticing. He looks like he just came from the beach or something. He's not very tall, but handsome nonetheless. He tried making small talk with me.

"You headed to lunch?" The mystery man asked.

"Yes, I actually am," I say while glancing up from my phone trying to act all *coy* and what not.

"I'm Chase McLaughlin. I think I've passed you in the office before, but I didn't know if it was the right time to introduce myself. I'm a graphic designer for Redbook magazine."

"Nice to meet you, Chase McLaughlin," I quietly murmur in an intrigued manner.

He's cute, but I don't really know what to say next.

"Would you possibly like to join me for lunch? I know we just met but, I thought I would ask since we might end up at the same place anyway."

I'm hesitant because I get really nervous around guys the first time we meet especially since we will be eating together. Yes, I'm THAT girl who doesn't like to eat in front of guys.

Of course, I panic and say, "Sure that sounds nice. Thanks."

We walk out of the building and walk towards our right. Chase asked if I like sushi and of course it is one of my favorite things to eat in the world. This place is a hole in the wall sushi bar called *"Sushi Zen."* It's small, but upscale looking with a reasonably priced menu.

This seems much like a date to me, but I have to realize guys can be just friends. This isn't the *When Harry Met Sally* generation. We sit down at a small two-top bamboo table, a little bonsai plant next to a tea light candle, and a lunch menu. The waitress came and took our order, and we decide to do a buy one roll, get one roll free. I'm glad to see that sushi restaurants here are similar to back home. This is going so smoothly. I'm waiting for a fiasco to happen.

"Do you like working for Cosmo?" Chase asked in a curious way as he put his napkin in his lap like a proper gentleman.

"I just started yesterday. I didn't get the chance to get lunch I was so busy. This is really nice of you to take me here. I feel like getting out really breaks up the day," I say as I tried to handle my chopsticks properly.

"I come here nearly twice a week because the price is right and it's not too far from the office. If you like it, maybe we can come again next Tuesday."

He showed me how to hold the chopsticks and explained it easier than anyone had ever tried. I even tried watching it on YouTube and could never quite get the gist of it. He seems genuinely nice. I'm starting to realize there are more men in this world besides Hugh Hamilton.

We got our sushi rolls after waiting only fifteen minutes. They came out on these really cool bamboo-cutting boards that were specifically designed for a small order of sushi. We ordered complete opposite types of sushi, and both tried each other's order. Chase is an interesting guy that I could become close to fast. We talk about our backgrounds and where we are from. Chase is from Seattle; I tell him my aunt lives there too. He went to the University of Washington where he got a degree in graphic design and graduated two years ago- definitely closer to my age than Hugh.

"How did you like growing up in the South? I don't know anyone who lives there, but I hear it's really great," Chase questioned while mixing his wasabi in his soy sauce.

Something my dad did to make it spicier but I had never seen anyone else do this. I said I liked it and moved on to the next subject really fast. I'm not good at this twenty-one questions game.

"Where is your place in the city? Do you like it here on the East coast?" I ask hoping we could talk more about where we were from.

Something I *do* know about.

"I love it here. It sucks in the winter how cold it is, but it's not much different than home in terms of weather. When I applied, I was supposed to work in the Los Angeles office, but they switched me here at the last minute really throwing my plan of tanning at the beach during my lunch. The city is great even though it's true what they say about it never sleeping. It's quiet where I lived in Seattle. It's pretty loud where I live here in Chelsea. I have a studio apartment above a cool new restaurant, but it makes for a noisy place to sleep. The owner of the restaurant owns my place; he cut me a deal on rent because they knew I would have to deal with loud pots and pans banging late at night."

Chase is the type of guy you *should* date but usually didn't. He's easy to talk to and very friendly. It's nice to meet new people because I hardly know anyone in this city.

"That sounds fantastic. I haven't been to Chelsea yet. Maybe you could show me around."

He was smiling a lot at lunch and laughing at what I was saying. It's easy to see that we have chemistry, but I'm not sure I should get roped into this so soon.

"I don't mind showing you around. What are you doing this weekend?" Chase asked in an optimistic tone of voice probably hoping I will be free.

"I'm not sure. But that would be fun. Hopefully, won't be babysitting." I say trying not to sound *too* available.

"If you're able to hang out Saturday, text me Friday night," he said as he put his number in my phone along with his e-mail.

We walk back to our building and take the elevator together. We talk about music and bands that we like. We have a lot in common which is rare for me to have with a guy. He isn't really my type, but I figure I will just see where the chips fall. I decide it's good to have a friend right now. Someone I can trust in the office and someone to go to lunch with. He showed me where Redbook is in comparison to my office, and we are pretty close in proximity. I don't think I will bump into him as much as I might with Hugh.

"Talk to you later, Scarlett!" he said while walking towards his desk.

"You too, Chase, thanks again for taking me to sushi, it was really good," I say kindly as I walk back towards my office.

It's half past one when I realize I hadn't prepared any questions for this girl I'm interviewing about the jewelry. I sit down and jot a few notes into my journal that I bought last night at Duane Reade. I went to the front of the office to greet her and show her to the conference room.

"Scarlett?" She said in surprised tone of voice as she went to shake my hand, which turned into an awkward hug.

Shit. Shit. Shit. Shit. I recognized her as soon as I saw her walk through the glass doors. She's a girl from my design class at CofC. I didn't know her last name yesterday when we talked, so I didn't think anything of it when I spoke to her on the phone.

"Oh my goodness, what are you doing here, Julie? I didn't realize the Julie I was speaking to on the phone was Julie Parker!!" I say excitedly trying to act stunned which isn't hard to do since I am.

"I'm now working for the jewelry line full time. I interned with them before our senior year. I got offered a job at the end of my internship. What are you doing here?" Julie asked in a valley girl kind of way that annoyed me as much now as it did when we had a class together.

She wasn't one of my friends in school, to be honest. She was one of the sorority girls that I had the pleasure of knowing since she was in half of my textile classes. She's the kind of acquaintance you're fake-nice to but really don't want to cozy up and share your life story.

"Well, how great is that. I'm so glad I can interview someone I know. Follow me we are going into the Cosmo conference room."

I paraded her through my amazing office towards the conference room, and she seems in awe at how nice it is. I can sense that she didn't think I deserve a job like this. I'm quite thrilled that I can show her up. My job is most definitely better than hers.

I sat at the head of the table, *like a boss*, and she sat to my left. Julie showed me a few sample pieces from the line, and I took some notes as she talked. We tried to focus on the work, and I was really glad because if anyone overheard us talking about College of Charleston I was screwed.

I try to wrap this meeting up as fast as possible all while getting the information I need to write my segment. As we finish up, Julie tries to make small talk and asks me where I'm living.

"I'm living with some friends in Gramercy Park until I can move into my new place in November."

I don't want to tell her the whole truth because then I will sound like a total loser.

"Oh, that is such a nice area of town. I'm living on the Upper East Side with a girl from the company that I met during my internship. We should all go out some time for drinks!" Julie says as she puts her jewelry back in the black velvet case.

"Yea, totally let's do it. I don't have your number so just write it down, and I'll send you a text."

Of course, I didn't have her number, we weren't friends in school; but now that we are adults living in the same city we are suddenly BFF! I love how girls say they should do something together and never end up doing it. That's something my mom has done to women at the grocery store for years. "Oh hey Sandy! We should play doubles soon with Brenda and Carol!" and then never actually speak to them after she said it. It's kind of hilarious that I'm doing the same thing with Julie.

I walk her to the front, and we did the awkward hug again- very strange. After the elevator doors closed, and she was gone, I could finally let my guard down. I was certain she would let some kind of bomb explode, alerting the entire office that we graduated from College of Charleston together in the spring. Thank God she didn't, or I would be packing to go home tonight.

I walk back to my desk hoping to just finish this up and try to breathe a little. The rest of the day I focus on my article. I met with Cooper to show him my progress, and we put a rough draft together so we could show Courtney our work in the morning.

I want to impress Courtney since it's my first real assignment. I'm already feeling a sense of belonging here in the office. I'm wondering if I should text Chase to do something this weekend. I guess *I'll do it tomorrow*, the Scarlett O'Hara way.

Sixteen

NBD, Just Cartier

"Scarlett, I'm in the basement, can you bring Ben down here for me?" Lisa shouted from the basement stairs. She sounds a bit out of breath. I hadn't been in the door for five minutes, and I'm already being summoned. I notice Donald isn't home yet; usually, he's home earlier. I pick Ben out of his pack and play thing and put him on my hip to go to the basement. I actually haven't been down here yet for whatever reason.

I reach the bottom of the stairs and see Lisa stretching on the floor with another man that appears to be her personal trainer. They did have somewhat of a home gym down here as I suspected. It reminds me of the one in my house, but it is much nicer with newer equipment and better lighting. Something state of the art that you would see on an HGTV program. They have a big flat screen TV mounted in the corner of the room and a mini fridge underneath that's probably filled with cucumber water.

"Hey, baby! I didn't forget about you. I knew Scarlett would take good care of you while mommy has her Pilate's session," Lisa says to Ben in a baby voice as she kisses his forehead.

"Thank you for watching him, Scarlett. Donald will be home in an hour. He goes to his fantasy football group thing at this bar on Tuesday nights while I exercise," Lisa says like she's out of breath as she lunged forward into a downward dog position.

"No problem. I will take good care of him."

I guess she just expected I would be home to watch him. Not like I have plans or anything. My only plans are to make myself a healthy dinner and lounge the rest of the night. I am so exhausted from these past couple of days and tired of eating food with processed ingredients. The lunch I had with Chase is probably the healthiest thing I've had since I arrived in New York.

I figured Ben would be cranky right now being so close to dinner and bedtime, but he's really well behaved for me. I put him back in his little safe haven, and make my way in the kitchen to make some dinner for everyone. I thought it would be nice to give them a home cooked meal by yours truly. I hope they don't mind me using what is in the fridge to whip something up for the three of us.

I decided on a pasta dish that my family loves hoping it's not too unhealthy for Lisa. I'm hearing some loud noises coming from the basement, and I'm starting to wonder if it's the *exercise* or *"something"* else. Lisa's trainer looked quite attractive and much younger than she and Donald. I'm really starting to think they are in some kind of weird arrangement.

About half an hour after I start cooking, Donald stumbles in the front door in his work attire and throws his briefcase on the floor. His shirt is unbuttoned at the top all the way down to his chest hairs. I figure he is probably a little tipsy after going to his fantasy league thing or whatever. My guess is he got drunk to tolerate the fact that his wife is into her personal trainer who looked to be shy of twenty-five years old or so.

"WOW! What is that smell? I'm digging it. I never smell home cooked meals like this," Donald says as he grabs a beer out of the fridge.

"It's just chicken carbonara; I hope you and Lisa like it. My family loves this meal. I just figured I would try to help out around here. Lisa should be finishing her session really soon," I said while stirring the homemade Alfredo sauce.

"I can't wait to try it," he says as comes over near me and takes a spoon to the sauce and tells me it's to die for. I can smell the bourbon on his breath giving away the fact that he is hammered. I better finish this meal quickly so he can come to his senses and sober up.

Just as I think Donald and I can have a normal conversation and be comfortable around each other, he reaches in his briefcase and hands me a bright red box with the word, *Cartier* on it.

"It's for you. I thought you deserve something nice for the start of your new job," he said with his smoldering brown eyes.

It *sucks* that I *actually* think he is attractive. I don't mean to think about a married man like that, but he is quite charming and handsome.

"What in the world?! A watch? Donald! I can't accept this! It's way too nice. Nicer than any jewelry I own…" I said in a shocking manner, as my eyes became the size of the *salad plates.*

"Scarlett, clearly you can see we have the money. Lisa doesn't mind. She likes you and so do I. A lot"

"I don't know. Wow, it is gorgeous. I feel like it's too much, though," I say while dazzling over the new Movado watch with the diamond dial and shiny platinum band.

I went to give him a hug to thank him and just as I embrace him Lisa walks up the stairs with her trainer. It's a bit awkward, but she doesn't bat an eye as she walks him to the door.

"I'm going to shower really quickly. The food smells good thanks for cooking, Scarlett!" Lisa said in a sincere happy tone of voice.

I wonder what kind of *happy ending* she just received. I'm also wondering if she'll notice the watch or figure out that Donald just dropped God knows how much on it with their *black* card. I can't help but feel special the way he presented me with the watch while Lisa wasn't around. I shouldn't feel this way. He is practically a stranger; a man that I have known all of five days that gave me the nicest piece of jewelry I own.

"Donald, I can't thank you enough for the watch. I really don't feel like I deserve your kindness but I'm truly grateful," I said while prepping the Caesar salad.

"Scarlett, you are a great girl. I just feel like spoiling someone. Lisa doesn't even blink when I do nice things for her she just expects it. I love her, but she doesn't seem to appreciate me anymore." He said as he got another beer from the fridge.

I feel he is genuinely sad about his marriage. I hadn't sensed this yet, but it seems they are working through something I'm not privy to. I want him to tell me everything while Lisa is upstairs, but I don't want to betray her trust. It's not right for me to be accepting gifts and feeling smitten by her husband. I really hadn't felt this way about him yet but he is so much different when it's just him. He's different when he's not sober. I can't seem to figure out why he's getting so bombed tonight.

Lisa finally came downstairs to join us for dinner. She looks happy and free of stress. I put the watch back in the *Cartier* box in my purse in case it isn't supposed to be advertised that Donald got me a very expensive and luxurious watch. I pull the garlic bread out of the oven and slice it to place in a basket. Just the way my mom and dad always do it when we have a nice dinner. They have very nice kitchen utensils that are clearly from somewhere nice like Williams Sonoma or Pottery Barn. It's rare to have everything you need from inside the refrigerator and the cabinets.

We sit down around their farmhouse table, and Ben is in his high chair next to Lisa. They both thank me for cooking this *"amazing"* meal, and we start to eat and talk about our day. I'm thinking how well this day has gone and wondered what could go wrong because usually things don't pan out this well for me.

"So I saw you two hugging…what was that all about?" Lisa presumes curiously as she stopped eating to look at Donald and me.

I knew that she was brooding over *something*.

"Oh, Scarlett was just thanking me for letting her stay here. She is such a sweetheart for being so gracious isn't she?"

I'm thinking to myself: what the HELL is he doing lying to his wife about me right now. I figure I have to play along, or I will be sleeping on the stoop tonight.

"Yea, Lisa, you and Donald made my first week of work so accommodating and so smooth. I can't thank you enough," as I put my hand on top of hers to show affection similar to how I did with Donald.

Let's just pray she doesn't check their bank account this week, or *ever*. She reassures me that she is glad to have me staying with them and hopes that I can be happy living there while I do. I'm wondering what the time frame for my move will be. I feel like if Donald is gifting me Cartier on week one, what could it be on week four; diamond necklaces? A mink coat?

I can't decide if I should tell anyone about the watch because they will for sure tell me to give it back. The truth is I don't want to give it back. I can't wait to flaunt it at work tomorrow and be well dressed for my meeting with Cooper and Courtney. I guess it won't hurt to keep this to myself for a little while.

Seventeen

What Would Katniss Do?

As I step onto the platform of the subway, I notice everyone is in a bit of a panic today. I have a big morning, and I really don't want anything to slow me down. The train finally approached, and I feel like I'm in a sea of angry, impatient, and intolerant crazy people. I had to force myself onto the train, pushing a few people out of the way. It isn't the time for me to be cordial. I can't be late because I have to meet with Cooper at nine this morning before we sit down with *'the boss'*. Nothing is going to ruin that for me.

Some very large African American girl who looked to be about thirty is sitting next to me holding her neon pink *Hello Kitty* backpack and her red drink. It literally says, "red drink" on the label. Her neck has a lovely tattoo with the script, *"Red Bone"* on it in big bold letters. I can only imagine how proud she made her mother with that decision.

A young guy, maybe eighteen, in clothes from the night before I suspect, is standing up eating a big can of Pringles and getting crumbs everywhere as he kept missing his face. I think he was probably hung over if I had to guess. I think his stench is the lovely booze aroma filling the train this morning. I think his scent is most likely conducive to the binge drinking he probably did the night before.

There's also a lady on the phone bitching out her hair salon saying how *Megan* screwed up her hair, and she won't be able to grow it back for months. She sounds very pissed. I'm going to have to remember never to go to a stylist named Megan while living here. I do however need to find a hair salon with someone who I can trust. Blonde is a hard color to get right it seems. It's either too blonde or too brassy from the experiences I've had in the past.

"Sorry for the delay folks, we are waiting for the other train to pass before we can go. It will only be a five-minute delay, thank you for your understanding," the conductor announces in an apologetic tone of voice.

It's not like I was on a deadline or anything. The amount of rolled eyes and ticked off huffing and puffing sounds coming from in my section of the train is outstanding. Five minutes can make or break being on time to work. Nobody is ok with this delay; it's as if everyone was woken up at four this morning by an infant crying and running low on sleep and patience. Oh wait, that's just me. I'm so ready to move into my own place so I can have some freedom to sleep as I wish and not answer to *anyone*. Lisa asked me to babysit Ben on Saturday night so she and Donald could go out and pretend to like one another. I guess if I do hang out with Chase it will have to be a daytime ordeal because I can't say no to Lisa. Not after how guilty I felt about the amazing watch that I'm currently staring down at hoping five minutes has passed so I can get to my JOB!

Many moons later, we finally reach our destination, and I exit the platform and rush up the stairs of the subway station. I always feel like I'm in some alternate universe when I finally reach fresh air. The *cold*, fresh air might I add. It's starting to feel like winter, and it's only the middle of October. I really need to consider bringing a pair of Uggs with me from now on, so I don't freeze on the way to work. My feet are numb from being so cold running around in the underworld. I haven't had much use for my boots until now. I never wore them at home, so they look brand new.

Finally, I'm on my crowded elevator full of even more annoyed executives, where every number looked to be lit up, I knew this day wasn't going to go my way. I'm ready to bitch slap someone into the next millennium at this point. I'm starting to think mercury is in retrograde or something; where everything that can go wrong will go wrong for the next few weeks.

I hadn't put anything together on my end because Cooper said we needed to collaborate first. So now that it's eight thirty-six, I'm officially late, and I feel screwed. We finally reach the twenty-sixth floor, and I didn't even stop to say hello to the receptionist, Sarah, whose name I finally caught yesterday after meeting her several times in passing since I started working here. I breeze by everyone and run to my cube hoping I have enough time to check my e-mails and meet with Cooper before our meeting with Courtney.

I log onto my desktop and get on the e-mail network and see this:

Good Morning Scarlett & Cooper,

Something came up with an issue for our sex and relationships segment coming out for the December issue. Apparently our writer has "Mono" or something dreadful. I have to go to a meeting and won't be able to meet with you until 3pm today. I'll see you both in the conference room then. Don't be late, please.

-Courtney

This e-mail is manna from heaven. I definitely need the extra time to sit down and really make this a good meeting. Thankfully my morning isn't indicative of what the rest of my day will be. I think this means things will look up for me.

I call Cooper, and we are able to meet in the break room for some much-needed coffee and discussion. I need something stronger than coffee today to handle the stress of my morning. Not to mention I'm officially exhausted and racking up a huge sleep debt living at the Quinlan's.

As we sit together sipping our espressos and deciding the final layout for our segment, Hugh parades in. I swear his timing is impeccable and also *super* off putting. I forgot he comes in here every day around ten, so it's not like he's doing it on purpose. "Wow, looks like you two have put together an awesome segment," he says leaning over the table while waiting for the machine to spew out whatever flavor coffee he decided on today.

"Thanks, good morning," I said with just a glance at his flawless clear blue eyes.

"I think if you moved the necklace to the center it would create a better visual for your readers."

I'm not in the mood to argue, but maybe he's right. I have to think of it as healthy criticism, and he is trying to help. Cooper agrees with him, therefore, we make the change.

"Scarlett, would you like to join me for drinks after work tonight?

I realize we haven't had the chance to get to know one another yet," he said in his oh so charming *Aussie* accent.

I feel kind of bad like I'm cheating on Chase even though I'm not even dating him. I just know I'm digging myself a big pile of shit with this.

"Umm, yea sure that sounds cool. Where do you want to meet up?"

I can't contain my excitement. I can't believe he asked me in front of Cooper. I'm sure Hugh doesn't mind because Cooper is gay if I had to bet my life savings on it. I really like Cooper so it would be kind of cool to have a gay friend in the city. It will be like Carrie and Stanford or Will and Grace.

"I'll just surprise you. I'll pick you up at your desk a little before five," he says as he sips his latte with whipped cream.

If he only knew what I wanted to do with him with that whipped cream, he'd probably reconsider our drinks tonight and take me right to his place.

Not only am I totally having a hard time concentrating on the rest of the afternoon, Chase asks me to go to lunch via text to make things worse.

"Hey, lunch buddy! Would you want to try this cool Indian restaurant I've been dying to go to?"

I don't really know how to feel about going to lunch with Chase AND drinks with Hugh later. I told him I have a deadline to meet and ask for a rain check. He seemed bummed in his text when all his reply said was, "Oh ok, well another time." I can't please all these men that are throwing themselves at me. I'm only *one* girl you know.

I wish I had time to go to the house and run a curling iron through my hair and change into something more appropriate to go out with the hottest guy I know. I could just meet Hugh there, but I don't want to look like I'm trying too hard if I change my outfit. This outfit will have to do. I can run to the Duane Reade during lunch and buy some makeup. Might not be a bad idea to have emergency mascara and blush at the office. I can splurge just this one time considering the extenuating circumstances.

I'm finally able to calm my nerves. I have a hard time not thinking I'm special for Hugh to ask me out on a *surprise* destination date. I really feel like ever since we met at the airport, we had a connection. I feel sparks every time I'm around him my heart literally feels like it's going to pound out of my chest. I haven't felt this way towards a guy *ever*. I'm not really the relationship or dating type. I wanted to get through college in four years, and that's what I did. Sure, I had guys that I liked or crushed on. Some that even took me to the movies or dinner, but nothing serious ever amounted. I can really see potential with Hugh.

"Time for our meeting, Scarlett," Cooper says as he sat on the corner of my desk with his *very* skinny jeans and tight black vest with suspenders. He dresses really well, but I'm not sure I can get used to the tightness of his clothing. He's a small guy, so it probably fit him best. It just seems like he gets his clothes in the little boys section at Macy's.

"Ok! I guess it's now or never. I hope this goes well!"

I close my planner and get up from my hot pink swivel chair. I don't know why but Courtney intimidates the hell out of me. It might be her Gucci bag and expensive clothes or her very sleek haircut that really bothers me. I think her confidence comes off as arrogance sometimes. I know I'm not the only one scared of her. She's not one to sugar coat anything.

We walk to the conference room and sit down across from one another allowing Courtney the "boss" chair at the head of the table. We thought it best to let her feel like the queen in charge of this meeting.

"I hope this is good because I only have fifteen minutes to get to my next appointment on time, and it's uptown," Courtney said exasperated as she threw her bags on the floor and brought her IPad on the table to take notes.

We give her the rundown of our segment, and I explain how I met with Julie, someone I could trust from the line and Courtney is pleased.

"*Loving* the placement of the necklace; it really catches my eye. Well done you two."

Thank you, Hugh, for that little-added idea today. We discussed a few minor changes on my end and decided to bold a few more things and alter the color a bit, but overall she likes it. I'm so happy right now that I pleased my boss. I'm curious as to what my next piece will be.

"Scarlett, since Macy has Mono or *whatever*, we need you to step in for her segment that is due in two weeks for our December issue. I hope that won't be a problem for you being that you're in our fashion department," Courtney says, as she looks at me with wide eyes hopeful that I'd be ok with it. I'm totally not ok with it considering I am not a sex guru AT ALL.

"Sure, Courtney. I can fill in for Macy if that is what you need. Just give me her contact information so I can see some of the ways she styles her segments. I will just need a few tips since this is not my area of expertise."

I hate saying that but I really have no idea where to start.

"Ok, I will give you her information, but I depending on you to make this happen. It doesn't have to be like her work. This segment is "How to Land a Holiday Hook-Up," just put your own creative juices to the test," she said.

Wow. Creative juices for a sex segment…a little uncanny hearing that given the topic. I guess I will have to see what I can come up with. Hopefully, I won't have to land my own hook-up to make this seem authentic, *"May the odds forever be in my favor."*

Eighteen

The Rooftop

Sometimes I wonder, why me? I can't understand for the life of me why Courtney would assign this segment to ME. Of all the writers at this company to sub for Macy she chose *me*. Part of me is wondering if she is testing me. She wants to prove I'm a phony and call me out on it by exploiting me with this awkward sex piece I have to write. Who knows, though; perhaps she is giving it to me because I did a great job with the jewelry piece. I have to think positively here, or I'll go full on crazy over-thinking things.

It's almost time to leave work and I totally just remembered my outing with Hugh. I rush to the bathroom to put on lip-gloss and check my hair. I have some deodorant and a trial size perfume in my purse that I use to freshen up as well. The idea of this has me sweating profusely thinking about it. I don't know why it's so important for me to look all "beautiful" and smell nice considering this is NOT a date. I know I say that this isn't the *When Harry Met Sally* generation, but I really feel like I can't be "just friends" with Hugh. I might be wrong about my theory that it's a *new era* and men *can be* friends with women. If it were the case, divorce rates in America would be much lower.

As I wait for Hugh, I look through a pile of old Cosmo's looking for a good example of the type of article I need to write. I use my hot pink highlighter and make some notes. I'm trying to occupy my mind so that five o'clock would roll around sooner. I had about fifteen minutes until that was to happen but it felt more like an eternity.

I want this article to be original, not like anything Macy has written before or anyone else for that matter. I just feel that most of my writing comes from true experiences. I don't want people to know I actually hooked up with guys to help fuel my article. I'm at the age now where you don't just have *flings*. My mom has always emphasized the "every date is a potential mate" concept, and I'm starting to wonder if she's right. I could just do a poll with some of the girls in the office. I doubt anyone is going to give out a random sampling of their latest hook up and walk of shame stories from last weekend. Why would anyone be open to that?

"Guess who," says a deep voice with an incredibly sexy accent behind me as his big hands cover my eyes.

"Hmm...I can't imagine who it could be," I say sarcastically as I turned around out of my chair.

"I hope you're ready to try the best cocktail in Manhattan, Ms. Hanes," Hugh says as he helps gather my things.

I wasn't ready for him. He was nearly four minutes early.

"After the day I've had, I'm ready to try the best *five* cocktails in Manhattan."

We walk together to the elevator, and I notice some glaring eyes from the other women who work here. *Clearly* Hugh is the office crush. It doesn't surprise me at all-I just ignore their envy.

Riding down the elevator, I can feel my heart racing, and I'm pretty sure everyone in here could hear it as well. I haven't been this nervous since my interview for this job! I have been waiting *weeks* to get a chance to be with Hugh, alone, and now that the time has come I want to crawl into a deep dark hole and hide. It just feels too easy and too good to be true to get to go on a little drink date alone with the man I have been crushing on since the day I laid eyes on him.

"I figured you wouldn't want to walk in heels, so I got a car for us," Hugh says so nonchalantly as if having a car service was no big deal.

The only car service I'm used to is Uber or a mini-van taxi. This is a black Mercedes-Benz with a driver wearing a suit, very swanky if you ask me.

"Well, that is awfully nice of you to do. My feet thank you!"

"It's no problem. The company gives me a stipend for travel each month, and I choose to use some of it for a car service. It's something I feel necessary with a *chocker* city and the traffic we have. It keeps my nerves calm, and it's not something I do every day. I just thought you'd enjoy it."

"What's a *chocker*?"

"Oh pardon my slang. It means *very full*. You know…like the city is full of a ton of people."

"I will agree with that. The traffic is awful where I'm from, but this takes the cake."

We sit in the backseat of the car and Hugh points to a couple of good places to eat along the way. Hopefully, he'll take me to dinner there sometime on a date. I can't help but feel the chemistry between us. Something about being alone with him outside the walls of our office feels so romantic.

We arrive to a five-star hotel, which has a rooftop terrace with views of the entire city. This guy already knows the way to my heart-a *rooftop* bar. I love a good view, and I haven't really had the opportunity to experience the nightlife of the city in the dark. The city all lit up is absolutely breath taking. I'm stunned at the views. Hugh is just enjoying watching me look at everything as if I'm a child who is at Disney Land for the first time. He ordered us the house cocktail, and we went to sit on the couches near the glass siding of the bar. I guess they have that for protection in case anyone gets over served and decides to topple over.

"How do you like the drink?" Hugh says as he sips out of the frosted martini glass with the lemon peel sliver for added décor.

"I think it's wonderful. You could have served me any generic beer and I would have been happy just to be here. I appreciate a good view."

"I'm so glad you like it here. I've only been here a few times but every time I do it impresses my guests quite nicely."

I'm sure it *impresses* the ladies. I wonder how many Hugh swoons his date with the nice little *car service* and the amazing lemon peel martini. I wasn't feeling so special after all.

"So who have you brought up here?" I ask casually hoping he wouldn't sense the bitter tone in my voice.

"I've brought some other photographers from the magazine and my brother in July for Independence Day."

That's a relief. I'm hoping he's not lying to me, but I don't see why he would. I have a hard time trusting men for whatever reason. I guess I've never really had a relationship work in the past. I have to remember that we are here as just friends.

"Scarlett, I have to admit something to you. I haven't been able to get you out of my mind since we met at the airport a few weeks ago. I'm very curious about you."

"Is that a fact? You haven't been able to stop thinking about me, but don't you have a girlfriend?"

"I did, but we're not in a relationship anymore. We live in different states. We both travel. I promise you I wouldn't be here with you if I weren't single." He said with sincerity in his voice.

"So you think you like me? Do guys like you even do monogamous relationships?"

"I'm pretty old-fashioned when it comes to dating, so I make sure I really like the girl first. I like to get to know the person first. Become friends before I get into bed with the girl."

"I can respect that. I'm the same way," I say as I finish my martini.

"Would you like another drink? We can try one of my favorite drinks if you'd like?"

"Yea, I think I'm going to need more than one drink to try and wrap my head around this situation. I like you Hugh, a lot. I have since we met. I don't like to admit that because I know I'm supposed to act all nonchalant, but I *like* you. I just worry that guys like you don't go for girls like me."

"What do you mean, girls like you? You are incredible, Scarlett. The fact you don't realize it makes you that more intriguing. Let's enjoy the night and get to know each other better before you write the script for yourself," he said as he got up to go retrieve more cocktails.

I guess my conscious is getting to me. I'm keeping such a big secret from him. Technically I haven't lied to him about my resume since he doesn't actually know my credentials. I haven't really lied about my roommates either I've just chosen to not disclose every single detail.

I look around the bar and notice almost everyone is coupled off. Seems like the kind of bar you bring your mistress to. I feel like I should end this before it goes too far. I don't want to lie to him. On the other hand, I could really use some dating experience for my column that I so happily get to write for Macy.

Hugh and I are feeling a little less tense after far too many cocktails, so we start opening up to one another. He told me about his siblings and childhood and where he grew up in Brisbane. The only outback I've been to is the one that serves blooming onions. Hopefully I'll get to go to Australia one day.

Hugh seems like the perfect gentleman really. I hate how much I'm drawn to his voice. They say an accent is a real deal breaker, and I get what they mean by that. I try to imagine him with a normal accent and I still really enjoy his presence regardless. He's funny and smart with a quick wit. We have so many common interests. Things always sound better after a few drinks, though. Life suddenly makes sense and the planets align. He seems passionate about what he does, and he really likes his job. There is literally nothing I don't like about him.

We didn't want to leave, but it was getting late. Hugh closed our tab and paid for our drinks, as a true gentleman would do. I gather my things, and he guides me through the door with his hand on my lower back. It's weird how such a small gesture aroused me. I can't help but want more. We are the only ones on the elevator going down thirty stories. That could give us time for just about anything.

"Scarlett, please don't take what I'm about to do the wrong way. I can't resist you."

Just as he finished his sentence, he was pulling me into his pelvis, cupping my face, and kissing my lips. I can't believe it. Hugh, the man I can't stop thinking about wants me. His lips are like soft, warm, pillows of sexuality. His arms were strong, and his breath was warm and minty. I think he has some kind of vanilla moisturizer on his lips to make things more delicious. I never want this elevator to stop.

"Holy smokes. You're a great kisser. I think we should try that again just to confirm," I say as I plant one on him.

Feeling the liquid courage right about now. I made a move on him and pulled him in wrapping my hands around his skinny waist. This is the most *sensual* experience I've *ever* had. Unfortunately, we make it to the lobby, and I know that we were done with our romantic outing.

"Thank you for a lovely evening. I really should be getting home now. I don't want to worry my roommates too much."

"You sure you don't want to get some food? I feel bad we didn't even eat dinner, and it's so late," he said in a concerned voice as he dials his driver."I really should get back. Maybe another time," I said checking my phone.

I hadn't checked my phone since we arrived. I had eight texts from Lisa wondering about dinner and if I would be home soon. I had one from Donald saying he and Lisa were trying to make sure I was okay because they hadn't heard from me in hours. I'm seriously about to lose my buzz for having to answer to these people. I think it's time for me to move out and be independent. I don't want Hugh to know I'm living with a married couple and a baby so I just tell him I will see him soon.

"I wonder if I might be too forward to ask if you would go to dinner with me Saturday."

I realized as he asked his charming question that I was supposed to tour the city with Chase on Saturday during the day and watch Ben at night for Lisa and Donald's date. I think it would be good not to be too available for Hugh. I don't want this to be too easy or predictable.

"I actually have plans on Saturday, but perhaps we could do next week sometime?"

"It's a date," he said as he kissed my cheek and put me in a cab to go home. He handed the driver a twenty-dollar bill to pay for my ride. He told the driver to drive careful. I could get used to this.

His scent is so *intoxicating*, and I NEED to go home with him. It's not like me to be so forward, but he has a strange effect on me.

How can I even think straight after what just happened? My life is becoming more interesting as the days go by, but I don't hate it at all. In fact, I'm really starting to love my life more than I ever thought I could.

Nineteen

Two Can Keep a Secret

I don't think I've snuck back into a house after going out except for mine, and that was when I was fifteen and didn't know any better. I didn't want to wake the baby up or Lisa and Donald. I disarmed the alarm and hoped they didn't hear me. It was close to midnight and I was exhausted and wondering how I would make it through the day tomorrow on five hours of sleep.

"Scarlett? Is that you? What's all the commotion down there? Can I help you get something?" Donald asks with a concerned voice as he came into the kitchen wearing nothing but Nike sweatpants.

His hair is all tousled like he's been sleeping for hours. I'm trying not to find him attractive, but there's something odd about the way he made me feel every time we were alone like this.

"I'm so sorry. I hope I didn't wake you guys. I had a work thing, and I didn't expect to get home so late. I just wanted to make a little snack, so I don't wake up feeling hung over in the morning."

I'm speaking in a quiet whisper, to ensure I don't wake Lisa. This would become a full-on awkward event if I had both parents lecturing me. Donald isn't really lecturing me, though, it seems like he's actually happy to see me.

"Why don't I make you some scrambled eggs or something? You smell like you've been in the liquor. Did you have a fun time?"

Donald is quite charming. He doesn't realize how sweet he is, and I'm sure Lisa doesn't realize it either. I feel like I'm having an emotional affair with a married man but I'm literally doing nothing. I just secretly find him attractive but even thinking this way has me feeling like I'm betraying Lisa.

I just left my wonderful date with Hugh, and now I'm on to the dad. I think this is what happens when you don't ever have a serious relationship, and then men suddenly pour into your life, and you just happen to like all of them at one time because the attention feels *really* good. Donald is married to Lisa and the father to a newborn. I wonder what my best friend would think of this. I wish I had her here to confide in-she's the only person that knows the real Scarlett Hanes. I need her to dish out all my dirty secrets to and drink strawberry margaritas.

"Thank you for cooking. I always feel better after eating when I go out. I would have had Shake Shack, but it was too far out of the way. I hope this doesn't make you groggy in the morning from being up so late."

I'm sincere. I feel guilty having Donald cook me a meal to sober me up from my sexy drunken night out with Hugh when I told him I was "working."

"It's seriously no problem. I will be honest with you; I haven't really been sleeping all that great since you moved in across the hall. It's not that you're bothersome, I just find something about you very intriguing, and I can't put my finger on it," he said as he scrambled my eggs.

I didn't really know how to respond to that. Frankly I don't feel comfortable telling him I feel the same even though the feeling is *quite* mutual.

"Is it possible that having me in the house is becoming a distraction from your marriage? I don't want to come between you and Lisa."

I don't have much of a filter when I'm drunk, so I just let that word vomit fall out of my mouth like it was no big deal.

"Nothing is going to come between us that hasn't already. Our marriage has been so different since Lisa got pregnant. We had to do several rounds of IVF, and the process put a real strain on our relationship. Things haven't been quite the same since. We have started to try different methods in our marriage; we even went to counseling. I know she has a thing for her personal trainer, but I just let it happen. To say I've become morose and withdrawn is an understatement. There are some things in life not worth fighting over."

I could sense the slight melancholy in his voice. He had the perfect marriage before their child, and now things are strained. I really don't think I came into their lives at the right time. I wish I could somehow help them rekindle their love. I guess I will just keep this to myself. No need to stir the pot.

"I'm really sorry to hear that, Donald; if there is anything I can do, please tell me and I will try. I hope your date on Saturday will help absolve some of your stress."

"I really appreciate you trying, you're really considerate- but I don't know if it will ever be the same. Scarlett, you're such a beautiful girl inside and out. I know any guy will be lucky to have you as their significant other," he said as he softly touched my cheek in a weird, yet endearing way. It made me feel kind of awkward but at the same time it was very comforting and assuring.

"That is really kind of you to say, Donald. I think Lisa is *lucky* to have you." I try to eat my eggs quickly and chug this orange juice so I can finally go to bed. I'm afraid what will happen if I stay down here any longer. I don't want to be the reason for the Quinlan's *divorce*. I'm not ready to take responsibility for something like that. I thank Donald and put my dishes in the sink. I tell him goodnight, and rush up the stairs as quietly as possible and get ready for bed.

I never quite understood the acronym, "TGIF" and why people always said it until now. Working hard during the week and not having any time to myself is something I'm not really accustomed to. I had it pretty easy back at home, and now I'm a full-time career woman. I'm wondering if Chase had remembered me asking him to show me the city the other day and I was wondering if I even wanted to do it. I'm so smitten with Hugh I feel weird going out with someone else. I need to try though because Hugh made it very clear that he wasn't going to settle down with anyone fast. I need to go out with Chase and give him a chance.

The entire morning has nearly flown by, and I haven't even thought about what I will do for lunch. I wasn't feeling my best this morning and didn't have much time to get ready since I pressed snooze three times. I skipped coffee because I'm trying to lay low and not run into Hugh or Chase in the break room.

"Hi! I was wondering if you wanted to go to lunch with me today," asked Cabot, whom I hadn't really spoken to since the beginning of my week. She snuck up behind me while I was typing away on my Mac. I was wondering when I might run into her. I guess it would be nice to have a girlfriend in the office, and I did need to go to lunch.

"Yea, that sounds great. I would love to."

I told her I would meet her in the lobby at noon, and she could pick the place. I'm a little nervous but elated that she wanted to eat with me. I need one on one girl time since Lisa isn't exactly in the same boat as me —age wise that is.

We both spot one another in the lobby wearing our very similar black trench coats and our very similar Tory Burch bags. Maybe we will have a lot in common besides our fashion sense. She seems like a nice girl, and I don't have many girls to lean on these days since Addison is so busy with school to even pick up the phone to call me back. I was afraid this would happen to our friendship; that it would fizzle out as soon as she got to law school. My predictions were starting to become a reality.

"I thought I would take you to this cute little deli around the corner. I don't think we should venture off too far considering the rain is going to ruin our hair if we do," she said as she directed me just to the left of our building about a block away.

We arrive at the deli, and it does have a nice little charming ambiance to it. It's small and seems packed full of young executives, mainly women our age. This must be the hangout women go to during lunch to gossip about their awful boss and coworkers. I'm surprised to see this many people leaving their desk with the weather the way it is. I've found that New Yorkers don't mind the crappy weather. I never want to leave the house in Charleston when it rains like this because it floods every time it rains. Something everyone from Charleston is used to.

We sit at a small table in the back corner up against the wall. It seems like Cabot doesn't want anyone to accidentally overhear our conversation. I feel like she wants to divulge all of her personal details because she doesn't know me well, and I can't judge her. People have a habit of self-disclosing their personal problems as if I'm some sort of therapist.

"I feel like I need to cut straight to it. I'm having the worst day of my life. I thought I could tell you because it seems like you're the type of girl that can keep a good *secret*."

I'm thinking to myself: if she only knew.

"Of course, I can. You can tell me anything I won't tell a soul. I promise."

"Scarlett, my fiancé and I just broke things off. I caught him talking to his ex from high school and found out it had been going on for quite some time behind my back. To make things worse, yesterday I picked up my *custom made* wedding gown from this designer boutique and they won't let me return it. I'm heartbroken."

"Cabot. I am *so* sorry to hear that. You must be devastated. I really hate that for you."

Well, my life doesn't seem *too* bad now after hearing that. I can't imagine what she is going through.

"I am. I live with Nate, and now I'm going to have to find a place to live. I love our apartment. He offered to move, but I think I need a fresh start. I don't want a reminder of what could have been, every single day. I don't know why this had to happen to me."

"Well, funny you are homeless because I'm actually in the market for a new apartment. I'm finding my roommates to be a bit too *noisy* these days and would really love to know someone from work better."

"Really? Would you want to maybe look for an apartment together? I know of this really awesome new luxury apartment building here in Mid Town that just started leasing last month. I tried to get Nate to move there, but he didn't think it was worth it."

"I'm totally down to look at it with you. I have a really busy weekend and work week coming up, but I'm free next Thursday after work if you are."

"That sounds awesome. I will contact the leasing agent for us and set up an appointment. I know we don't know each other well, but that could be good. I never pictured myself moving somewhere with anyone but Nate. I hope you're ready to make the most of my new life as a single girl. We will have to have a lot of fun to distract me!"

"I certainly agree."

After spending much of our lunch getting to know one another, I realized that Cabot and I would probably get along *swimmingly*. I'm excited to think about moving out of the Quinlan's because I'm serious about the *noise* factor. Ben is starting to teeth, and his screaming has me developing a bit of a hearing impairment. I'm nervous about Cabot getting too close to me and figuring out the truth. I couldn't figure out whom I could tell my secret to or if I could tell anyone at all.

I have to realize that I can't go the rest of my life worrying about my resume secret. I have to move on and not let it define me. I will tell the right people when the right time comes if it ever does. I don't want to hurt anyone so I will just have to keep personal things to myself that involve my past and work. Hopefully, we will just talk about relationships and makeup and men. I'm really starting to love my life, and I don't want it to all come unraveled. This is going to start a completely new chapter in my life: a new friend, a new apartment, and possibly a new relationship…

Twenty

Thank God It's Friday

Later that day at work I receive a visit from Chase at my desk. I wasn't expecting it, but I guess he was going to have to arrange our outing somehow. I was just expecting a text or something generic like a Facebook message. Most guys I ever went out with weren't much for grand gestures.

"Are you ready to see the city like you never have before?" He asked with a piece of paper in his hand that I was curiously staring at.

"Are you going to tell me what that is?" I ask pointing to the tan grainy scroll in his hand like a message in a bottle.

"This Scarlett is a to-do list for tomorrow. There are a few things I felt necessary for you to experience before you could truly call this your home."

I don't even know how to take this. It's nice but a bit overkill. Chase is the kind of guy that should get all the girls but probably doesn't because he tries so hard. I don't really get why girls operate this way, but we like to make things hard on ourselves; I sort of get why Rihanna went back with Chris Brown after he beat the shit out of her. We don't like nice boys; it's just how we're wired. I rolled out the scroll and read the bullet points off the list Chase had written down in permanent marker.

- Go to the Central Park Zoo,
- Get a cronut aka a croissant-donut they are amaze-balls
- Walk on the High Line

I guess these were cool things to do, and I hadn't been to any of these places yet, and I've definitely never had a croissant donut. I'm willing to take my chances and see where this leads.

"If you want, I can meet you at your place and pick you up in the morning around ten?" He said probably hoping I wouldn't reject him ruthlessly.

"Sure, I'll text you the address."

I'm not sure why, but I feel like I can tell Chase the truth about Lisa and Donald, and he won't judge me. I really do wish I could explain myself to just *one* person. Addison would most likely advise me to tell nobody, but she's not here, and she won't talk to me, so I have to listen to my instincts. I also want someone's opinion on living with a coworker. I won't tell everything to Chase, but I do think I can be selective with how I tell him.

After a grueling Friday, I decide to take it easy after a long workweek and take a much needed, very long piping hot shower. Lisa was visiting her aunt in New Jersey for the night, so it was just Donald, Ben, and I. Not sure I'm ok with this, but I enjoy Donald's company so it can't be that bad.

I want to figure out my outfit for tomorrow with Chase and clean up a bit. I have yet to do any laundry since I got here, and it's really starting to pile up-not to mention I don't have any clean underwear. I thought it's perfect timing while Lisa is gone. I didn't want her to ask me to do their laundry and sift through all of her thongs and Donald's briefs.

"Hey kid, come down here and watch a movie or something. Ben is asleep, I turned on the fire, and I'm bored," Donald shouts from the bottom of the stairs.

"I'll be right down I just need to call my mom and give her an update on my life."

I hadn't spoken to my mom other than a few texts since last weekend. I really am trying to distance myself, but it's so hard not leaning on her for things like I used to. We became so close this summer, and I felt like our relationship had grown into an adult kind of bond that you hope for when you're a teenager when you don't get along at all. I called her and spoke to her about my new sex piece that I'm supposed to write, the kiss with Hugh, getting an apartment with Cabot, going to tour the city with Chase and about to watch a movie with a married man. No, my life is not boring *at all*. I didn't mention the watch from Cartier because I thought that was something nobody really needed to know about. I will probably just tell my family I got it in China Town or something. She sounded really happy for me and seemed like she was happy too. She said that everything was going well, and everyone missed me, especially my grandfather. I feel bad I haven't called them but I will on Sunday night; that way I can tell them *all* about my weekend.

I put on my flannel pants and a gray oversized Columbia sweatshirt that Addison bought for me as a joke. She figured it was probably a staple that every girl from Columbia had, and I needed one to look the part. It felt really strange wearing it considering it was the only piece of that school I could truly own. I gathered my dirty laundry and took it to the washer and dryer they had in the hallway. After putting a load in, I went downstairs and made myself comfortable on the love seat with the really soft fur blanket that I lay claim to. There are some things that I will really miss when I move out. I'm wondering how soon that will actually be.

As Donald and I watched some romantic comedy, I thought about how my life isn't too far off. I feel like my life sounds normal in my head, but when I speak of it out loud, it sounds somewhat like a train wreck waiting to happen. I'm sitting here with a married man on a Friday night by the fire watching Netflix, drinking red wine, and eating popcorn. This seems wrong on all levels, but I'm really enjoying myself and relaxing for the first time all week. Donald allows me to be normal, and not place any pressure or demands that I'd face with a real date night. There'd be cuddling and making out, and God knows what else. The fact that he is married makes it easy for me to like him because he is a guy I know I can't have so I'm able to totally be myself when I'm around him. Sure, I like to look at him and occasionally flirt around, but I'm not going to do anything about it. That's what I like about him. He's like going to a fancy art museum with crazy sculptures and displays that won't let you touch them, but you can spend all day looking.

It's almost two in the morning, and Donald is sleeping on the couch, and I'm seriously tipsy at this point, so I need to go to bed. They drink the expensive wine on the top shelves at the store you can't imagine splurging on. I'm not sure if I should wake him to go to his room or just leave him there. Someone is going to have to take care of Ben at like four in the morning, and it's not going to be me. I have to get my beauty rest for my date with Chase. I'm not sure if we are considering this a date or not but it feels like one to me. Any time I'm going on a solo outing with a man at my age I consider it a date. I'm not just wasting my precious weekend with a man for no reason. If I actually wanted to see the city, I would just go with Cabot or Claire or even Lisa. So I'm trying to get my ducks in a row for this and I can't be distracted by a crying infant; I guess I should put the baby monitor directly in Donald's ear so he'll hear it when Ben starts screaming bloody murder for his morning breast milk. Lisa left several bottles of it in the fridge for Ben while she's away. She numbered them so we would know how much to feed him and when. I guess she doesn't trust us to keep a baby alive for twenty-four hours. I can't say I blame her because I'm no expert when it comes to babies and their feeding schedule.

I can't sleep because I'm worried about the baby across the hall, and I'm worried about everything going on in my life right now. I feel guilty even thinking about the apartment hunt with Cabot as I lay in this amazing bed the Quinlan's have so kindly provided for me. Surely they expect me to move out soon and start my life. I feel like I've grown so accustomed to being here even though it hasn't been very long. I guess I will scroll through my social media for the thousandth time and maybe my eyes will start to feel heavy. After perusing the online articles and checking the weather several times, I finally fell asleep. At three A.M. I'm not going to feel good for this outing. Hopefully, there will be coffee involved, and maybe he'll pick me up in a nice car like Hugh did. I doubt that, but a girl can dream.

Twenty - One

"Let's Get Physical, Physical"

Thankfully I was able to sleep until nine this morning. I didn't hear Ben screaming or Donald fussing with him, but I assume they are still alive. I decide to get up and shower so I can wash my hair and tame the beast. For whatever reason, I want to look hot, and I'm not even sure I'm attracted to this guy. I will use all of these dates as material for my column. Courtney didn't specifically say it was sex; she said holiday *hook-up* so it can be mild. I'm sure she wants the details to be juicy and vivid.

I'm not going to dress up, but straight hair and make-up is a must. I will wear my favorite Hudson jeans that hit right at my ankles, a loose v-neck shirt to show a *little* cleavage, and my army-green jacket with white Converse *obviously*. I want to look pretty but not like I'm trying too hard. Chase is kind of a simple guy with his appearance. He isn't like Hugh, who is obviously into fashion. I don't mind Chase's appearance; he just doesn't have any striking features so to speak.

"I'm on my way-I'll see you in fifteen minutes or so," says Chase in his text message.

"Ok, I'm here whenever you arrive just call me," I replied.

I grab my satchel and go downstairs to see what's up in the kitchen and hopefully grab some breakfast before he gets here. It appears that Donald and Ben are taking a mid-morning nap according to this note:

Scarlett, help yourself to some breakfast. Ben had me up pretty early this morning, so we decided to get some extra shut-eye before Lisa gets home. Have fun today and call me if you need rescuing-see you later.

-Donald

Well, that makes this easy. I grabbed a cold pressed green juice out of the fridge and chugged it down while reading the New Yorker on the table. It appears there is some kind of gay pride rally in the middle of the city today. I wonder what that will be like. I've never been to a rally, especially not one for the homosexuals.

I need to brush my teeth, and check my makeup one last time so I run upstairs quietly trying not to wake the baby. I run into Donald in the hall wearing nothing but his briefs once again half naked. It's really time for me to move out of here, so I don't have to witness this kind of thing anymore.

"Where are you headed looking all gorgeous?"

"I'm going to gallivant around the city with a colleague because apparently trying a *cronut* is a must," I say as I try not to stare at the bulge in his lower region.

"I agree with your colleague. Cronuts are worth the wait. Hope you have fun. See you later," he says as he walks downstairs with me.

I'm eager to leave the house, so I just walk out the front door and sit on the steps. I didn't expect to see Chase the way I did, but he was coming down the street in a little rickshaw thing I've seen downtown,

Charleston. I can't believe he's picking me up in one of these things. I'm pretty sure I've only been on one at two in the morning, and I was plastered. I guess this is my ride for the day.

"Good morning, Scarlett! Your chariot awaits you," he said as he got out of the rickshaw.

"Wow. This is quite the setup you have here. How did you manage this?"

"This is my buddy; he owns this rickshaw company, and he owed me a favor. I even brought a blanket because I thought it might get chilly riding around. We have him for four hours. I hope you are ready for the quintessential NYC experience."

This certainly surprises me. I want to think it's overkill, but I really think it's kind of romantic and thoughtful. Chase is the bi-polar opposite of Hugh. He is very avant-garde and eclectic. He has a certain bravado that I respect and want to learn more about. We both got settled in the little back seat of the carriage as I'm calling it, and we ride towards town.

"I hope you're ready to try the most delicious dessert you've ever had," he says as he slyly put his hand on my left thigh. I'm not going to stop him, or it will become awkward and possibly ruin the date.

"I've been told cronuts are really good. They better be worth all this hype," I said.

We arrive at "Dominique Ansel Bakery," and park a few blocks away. I can't figure out why until we get there. The line is wrapped around the entire corner of the building. Chase told me that they sell out of cronuts within thirty minutes of making them fresh every day. You have to get there right when they make them, or you will miss out. Apparently they make them early in the morning. It's a small window of time just to create supply and demand apparently.

"Umm, this is interesting…I hope you're right about these croissant donuts. I'm anxious now," I say as we stand at the back of the *very* long line.

"The line moves pretty fast-I remember being a skeptic my first time coming here. I couldn't believe anyone would wait this long for food."

I can believe people wait for food. My favorite restaurant downtown, Jestine's, is one of the best southern fried food joints downtown. It's a small hole in the wall corner restaurant that you wait outside until there is a table ready for you to come in. It's worth the wait because the food is out of this world. I would give anything for some of their pecan pie right now. If it's anything like Jestine's, it will be worth the wait.

"I'm not too worried. I trust you. It must be good or all of these people wouldn't be standing in the cold for it."

As we edge closer to the entrance, we notice the look of dismay on everyone's face coming out. Sheer disappointment and some downright pissed. We have waited nearly half an hour to find out they ran out of cronuts. I'm pretty ticked off myself considering everyone got me so excited, and now Chase feels bad, so this is starting off a little rocky, to say the least.

"I am so sorry. I will have to make this up to you somehow," he said apologetically.

"It's ok! What's on the agenda next?"

"I thought I would take you to the Central Park Zoo if you're interested?"

Truth is, I'm not exactly excited about spending the day with smelly animals, but I don't want to crush him after this letdown. I guess I will just keep my opinions to myself and let it ride.

"Sure, let's go."

We get back in the rickshaw and head uptown to Central Park. I did think it was pretty fun riding in this thing, but you stand out like a sore thumb.

On the way there, we got stuck in a bit of traffic due to the gay rally in Times Square. I'm rather intrigued and want to see all the action. I prefer this kind of thing to going to a dumb zoo.

"I wonder what's going on over there. I bet people are getting super weird," I said as I pointed to the crowd.

"I have seen one of these before. Things can get ugly if the cops shut them down. They don't like to be told no to anything," he said as he motioned for us to go a different way.

I guess I wasn't going to the rally today. I will have to see it another time. Apparently it's something that goes on in NYC regularly. I'm trying to be a team player, but I'm already kind of over this, to be frank.

"We're here. Just stay right here and I'll go buy us some tickets to get in," he said as he hopped out of the rickshaw.

At least he is buying the tickets. I saw a sign saying, twenty-dollars for adult's general admission. Everything is steep in NYC I can't afford it right now, that's for sure. I notice all the interesting people in the park and all the outlandish things they were doing. There's a lady painted a shiny light blue, silver color dressed up like Lady Liberty. I went up to her to take a picture, and she made me put this ridiculous American flag on with a crown while holding the statue with fake fire on top. I can't believe that she is doing this to me, but I just went with it. I see Chase coming towards us and hope that he has a sense of humor.

"HA, you look so hot right now. I should have warned you this might happen if you try to take a picture," Chase said as he got out his phone to snap a pic.

"Well, you left me here all alone and vulnerable to be taken advantage of," I said as I took off the ridiculous costume and handed it to Lady Liberty. She looked at me motioning to tip her for dressing me like this stupid clown. I wasn't going to hand her any money because she conned me into putting this get up on.

"I think I can cheer you up by taking you to the penguin exhibit. Who doesn't like penguins with their little tuxedos on?"

"You're right. I do love penguins," I say smirking at him. Chase looked awfully cute today with his big Ray-Ban sunglasses on and his tight jeans. He isn't very muscular, but he's definitely trim and attractive. I guess a little flirting wouldn't *kill* me.

We spent the afternoon looking at all the different species and animals at the zoo; I actually had a good time. I realized how hungry I was after walking around for nearly two hours. I'm hoping he'd offer to take me to lunch so I could give my legs a rest, and make up for not getting that delicious snack earlier.

"So I thought we could go to this spot around the corner from here. They have the best New York pizza you'll ever try; if you like pizza that is."

"Who doesn't like pizza? That is just criminal. Take me now!"

Our lunch that Chase bought for us consisted of two slices of "pie" and a couple strawberry-kiwi Snapple's. I noticed that everyone around the city drinks Snapple for whatever reason. I probably haven't had one of these sugar infested drinks since elementary school after a soccer game. It actually did pair nicely with the pizza. It's a cute little pizza place with red leather chairs and black and white checkered floor. There are pictures of what I think to be an Italian family all over the place; probably the family that owns the joint. It looks like it has been here for nearly fifty years and it probably has. I'm feeling pretty content at the moment. A good lunch and I was inside away from the cold weather. I say its cold, but it is only sixty degrees; pretty cold to me.

Chase wants to take me one last place; the Highline-he said it was something new that I probably hadn't seen yet since it was just built this past year. I was down for one last thing, and then I had to get back to babysit Ben for the night.

"I hope you're having a good time today. I know I am."

"I am. I really enjoyed watching the polar bears swim and the pizza was really good. I think you're a good tour guide," I said as I kissed him on the cheek.

"Why, thank you. I just wanted you to have a fun time," he said as slowly grabbed my hands and pulled me in close to him. He looked me in the eyes, put my hair behind my ear, and kissed my lips. I wasn't expecting a kiss out of him at all. Much less on the lips, pretty *bold* move. I'm not mad about it. I actually enjoyed it.

We had a weird connection at that very moment. I wanted more. I wanted to know what he is capable of. I want him to take me back to his apartment and roll around on his bed. I want to try more things with him. It's a different feeling with him than with Hugh. Obviously, I'm sober now, so there's that. I feel a weird connection with Chase. Sadly I think I need to experience the physical aspect with both guys to really rule out who would be a better match.

Once arriving at the Highline, Chase shows me the beautiful plants surrounding the place and the panoramic views from the walkway. The city is breath taking from here, and you can see everything. He grabs my hand and starts asking me about my life. I end up telling him a lot about me without giving everything away. I tell him about living with the Quinlan's, but not how we met. I just told them they were family friends.

I feel like I could talk to him for hours because he is such a good listener. He is the kind of guy you were *supposed* to be with. He is the kind of guy I want to get physical with because he has me so curious. He wants to know me. I want to know him. I'm now super torn between two incredible men. I want to get physical with Hugh, but that has been a given for a while. I know that the next time I'm with Hugh something will happen. I never thought I would have options the way I do now. After all, it's ok to date multiple men at one time according to my mother.

I get back to the brownstone around five just in time to allow Lisa and Donald to make their reservation across town. Chase was a gentleman and made sure I got home safely. We ended up taking a cab because our carriage turned into a pumpkin.

"Scarlett, we left some money for you to order take-out if you want anything to eat while we're gone. I left all the emergency numbers and contact info on the sticky note on the counter. Keep the baby monitor with you at all times when Ben falls asleep. We will be back around eleven tonight," Lisa announced as she and Donald walked out the door.

He glanced back at me as if he wanted some kind of approval for going out with his wife after telling me their marriage is in shambles. I feel kind of bad for him because I'm afraid they won't come back together, and he'd end up staying at a hotel or something.

"Have fun! We will be just fine here," I reassured them.

Frankly, I haven't babysat since high school, and I'm not too familiar with infants or all this new technology since I never really cared for them. I always babysat kids that were in elementary school or older because I felt like changing diapers was a dirty job. Now people have these crazy nanny cameras that spy on your kid's every move.

I figure Ben will go to sleep in a couple of hours, so it couldn't be too hard. I'll just feed him and put him in pajamas and hopefully not have to hear him cry all night for Lisa.

I texted with Chase for the majority of the night since Ben was asleep by eight. We were flirting with each other and talking about our next date which would hopefully be soon he said. I had totally forgotten about the dinner date I'm supposed to go on with Hugh and wondered if I even wanted to.

Donald and Lisa came in around eleven like they said and I had fallen asleep on the couch. I woke up when I heard the alarm being deactivated and saw them making out and rushing up the stairs like teenagers. I guess they don't feel the need to interact with me. I'm delighted that they rekindled their love, but it made me feel kind of awkward knowing they were about to have sex with me right downstairs below their bedroom. Not to mention their child is asleep in their room. In a way, I feel like this is a wake-up call for me. It's time for me to move out and I feel like I did my duty. I made them go on a date, and now they are happy. Everyone wins today.

Twenty - Two

"Hi"

The next few days flew by as I worked on my new segment. I'm starting to feel more connected to the piece after experiencing two different kisses with two different guys in one week. I needed to take it to the next base to have more lucrative information for an actual hook-up.

I have a lot on my plate and I need to get this done before next Friday when I am to give Courtney my rough draft. I'm supposed to tour the new apartment with Cabot after work tomorrow evening, and it totally slipped my mind. I'm managing to focus on my work being that I hadn't heard from Chase or Hugh this week. Waiting to hear from Hugh about our date is driving me ape shit.

I decide to take things into my own hands go to the break room at ten knowing Hugh would most likely be there. I know this might seem childish, but a guy can't leave a girl hanging for nearly a week and expect her to be ok with it. "Hi Scarlett, how are you?" Hugh seems startled. "This is Emma; she's here for a photo shoot for Elle's December issue," he said as he turned *Scarlett* red in the face.

"Nice to meet you, Emma. I'm doing fine, Hugh." I'm feeling like a jealous girlfriend, and I don't even go out with him. I get the sense that she has a thing for Hugh the way she is pawing all over him like a puppy. She is trying to send the message, "HE IS ALL MINE BITCH!"

I aim to leave as soon as my coffee is done brewing. I can't help but notice her beautiful features. She's *flawless*, and I hate to think that. I hate her. I wanted to scream but instead I said this:

"Hope you two have fun today. Hugh, can I speak with you out here about my *sex* segment?"

His eyes were wide open at this point. He knew what I was doing, and I don't even care at this point. I figure my chances with him are slim to none anyways. He met me in the hallway after telling Emma he would be right back.

"Scarlett, what's up? What can I help you with?" Hugh asked in a subdued and slightly perturbed voice.

"What is her deal? She is slobbering all over you. Have you two dated in the past?"

"She's being a brat today. She's leaving to go home tomorrow morning. I promise we will talk more then. I have to babysit her for a little longer."

I can't figure out if he was being real, or if he was just telling me what I wanted to hear. She's probably staying at his apartment tonight. Why would she feel the need to have a hotel room when she has her ex fling's place to stay? If I don't cool it, I will certainly lose my shit. I have to finish this piece, or I will indeed get fired.

Time has passed and I've cooled off a bit, so I decide to text Chase.

I figure he is a good distraction for what I'm going through right now. I have no idea what to say to him. I just keep it really simple:

"Hi," I say in my text. I wait for nearly twenty-five minutes for a response from him, and he finally says this back:

"Hi."

I can't believe we are being such children. I don't know what to say to him I don't want to ask him out. I know this is the twenty-first century, but I'm a Southern Belle and want to keep it that way. I don't say anything back and decide to let it play out. I wonder if he's going to respond or if we are just going to leave it at that. I sit at my desk typing out the outline for my piece when he comes to my desk.

"I decided to come by instead of text you back. I didn't really know what to say," he said while kneeling by my desk.

"I'm glad you did because I'm not exactly a wordsmith right now. I feel overwhelmed, and I just wanted to talk to a friend."

"What can I help you with?"

"Would you want to do something after work tonight?" I said hoping he would have a good idea because I don't.

"Sure, why don't you come over and I'll cook us dinner or something. We can just hang out and talk about work and watch a movie. Have a low key chill night."

"That sounds perfect. Just what I need right now," I said as I looked up at him giving him a slight smile.

Thankfully Courtney told everyone to leave early today. This hasn't happened yet, but I assume there is some kind of reasoning behind her kindness. She doesn't just give out freebies like this. I'll take it, though. I want to go home and change into something more appropriate for *"chilling"* with Chase. I think it will be nice to just relax and hang out. I can pretend I'm back home and not even think about being in this crazy dysfunctional city with my crazy dysfunctional life. I need some normal tonight. It's like Chase read my mind and granted my wish like a genie.

It's time to break out the Ugg boots and look totally cliché with my black leggings and oversized sweater. I want to be comfortable but look cute at the same time. Obviously, I'm wearing sexy underwear in case things heat up between us. I'm not even thinking about Hugh and Emma at this point. I'm excited to get a home cooked meal by a man that I thought to be pretty cute. I'm hopeful he'll be a good chef, so we don't end up at the restaurant below us.

I arrive in Chelsea where Chase lived around six trying to be casually late. I didn't want to get there right as he was getting home and be sitting outside his front door like a stage-five-clinger. Chase came down and let me in the door to his apartment. I did pass the restaurant on my way in and went up the very steep stairs to his loft. I'm glad he doesn't have a roommate. It seems like older guys are over the roommate scene. Unfortunately, I'm not able to swing that kind of deal just yet. Cabot and I will be living together soon if everything goes as planned tomorrow night.

"I hope you like Italian food. I made us chicken Parmesan," he said as he stirred the sauce.

"I love Italian food. You know the way to a girl's heart."

His place is tidy and cozy. It smells fresh too. I notice he has a lot of cool artwork around and come to find out he has a dog.

"You didn't tell me you had a dog! I love dogs!" I say as I kneel down on the hardwood floor to pet the loving animal.

"I'm sorry I forgot to mention that. She's a sweet girl. Her name is Scout; she's a labradoodle; she's only two years old."

"I *love* this breed. They're such good animals. They're really well behaved. Who takes care of her during the day?"

I could play with Scout all night I just love her. I think it would be really hard to have a big dog in the city. It's a huge responsibility and to live in a big city and work all day seems kind of unfair to the dog.

"I actually hired one of the servers that works in the restaurant to come let her out before her shift. She really likes Scout, so she doesn't even charge me."

I watch Chase cook the rest of our meal and drink the delicious craft beer he got for us. I'm not really into beer, especially with Italian food, but I think he's somewhat of a beer connoisseur. I felt really laid back in his apartment and really happy to be here. Everything is just fine until I get a text from Hugh.

"I'm sorry about today. I want to make it up to you--dinner Saturday night?"

I want to ignore him, but I feel bad. I was so mad at him today, and he probably felt like a dick after we talked. I wasn't trying to guilt him into liking me at all. I just wanted him to know I didn't like the way she was slobbering all over him right in front of me with no regard.

I told him he was going to have to really make it up to me for me to say yes. He said he promised he would, so I agreed. I feel like I constantly have to choose between him and Chase, but I have to do this to know what I want. In a way, I feel like I'm using Chase because I only texted him because I was mad at Hugh for not telling Emma to lay off.

I try to ignore the voices in my head telling me this is wrong and enjoy my dinner with Chase. Turns out he's actually a very good cook and I really like the dinner he made. I'm trying to think about literally anything except Hugh right now but I can't. I want him so much more knowing I can't have him right now. I can't even imagine what he and Emma are doing. I don't know how he got away with texting me while being with her. It's possible he doesn't like her, and it's just a one-sided thing.

"Do you want to go in my room and watch a movie?" Says Chase as he put our dishes in the sink.

I think this means we could get into *something*. Something I can't think about right now because my thoughts are consumed with the image of Hugh and that devil spawn.

"Yea, sure, let's *do it*."

I laugh after I say it. I didn't mean it that way obviously, but my mind was somewhere else.

"Sounds *good* to me," he says laughing and smiling as if he really wants it.

He turned on an old Adam Sandler movie and curled up next to me when he told me he couldn't pay attention anymore; that I was too pretty to focus on a dumb movie.

He put his hands under my sweater and slowly guided his hands to the lower part of my back. I can tell he is eager to do more, but I don't know what I should do. I guess I should just let it play out and use some of this for my segment at work.

His breath fanned my face, and it smelled like hoppy craft beer, he must have been drinking before I got there to ease his nerves. He came towards me and pulled me close. I was now straddling him and knew it was going to go further than first base. For whatever reason, I'm excited to be moving to the next level with him; I wanted to know more. I wanted to know what kind of physical chemistry we have.

We start making out and *French* kissing. His hands are slowly going up my sweater to my bra when I noticed he had unclasped it. I didn't even care. I just let it happen. I wanted Chase to feel my breast and touch my skin. I wanted him to slide my leggings off and throw them on the floor. So he *did*.

We are both half naked at this point, and he has seen me without my top on. I'm still wearing my boy shorts, and he is in his boxers, and I'm wondering how far this should go. We roll around on the bed making out like wild animals at this point. He is such a good kisser and knows exactly where to put his hands. I'm really turned on, but I feel like I should stop this before we go too far too soon. If this was Hugh, I might let it go all the way, but I don't want to lead Chase on if I do happen to like Hugh more. I can't sleep with two guys in a week.

"I think we should wait. We don't have to rush things. We should just let this be easy for a little longer," I say grabbing the blanket to cover my body.

"Ok, I understand…but you don't have to put your clothes back on. You look so sexy like this." I didn't want to stop. I *sort of* like Chase, and I didn't really realize that until right now; he knew what to do to get me excited. Courtney did tell me to let my "juices" flow…I didn't want to use Chase as a work experiment, but he was certainly doing a splendid job. We continue to make out and flirt for the next hour or so. There's so much sexual frustration going on in here. "I think I should head home. It's getting late, and I don't know how much more of this I can handle without going further," I gasp while grabbing my clothes and getting dressed.

"We can save the rest for *next* time. I had a really fun night with you, Scarlett. You are some kind of amazing, girl."

I got in a cab and went back to Gramercy. I don't feel like riding the subway I already feel dirty after what just occurred. I just left Chase, but all I can think about is going to Hugh's place to see if he was shacked up with Emma. I know I have to let it go, or it will kill my mood. It's so weird how I feel about Chase after what I just did. It's very out of character for me to hook up with a guy I barely know. I still don't feel that spark with him the way I do when I'm around Hugh. Something tells me that I'll never get over Hugh until I get *under* him. That sounds awful, but I do feel it's true. I feel such a rush when I'm with Hugh. Even if it's just watching him pour coffee into his mug; everything he does is enticing. I like Chase, but I feel like there's something missing there. Maybe he's just not the guy for me. I know he's the right guy for some girl out there.

I decide to call Addison on my way home and give her the nitty-gritty. We talk for nearly the entire cab ride; I can't believe she even picked up for me. She seems pretty surprised by my love affairs. She was too busy with school and trying to land an internship for the spring semester to have any fun. It's as if we have traded roles. I'm glad to be the one having a good time for once. She was proud of me for sticking to my guns and not going all the way. The cabbie was probably sitting in the front thinking I'm some kind of whore. I don't even *care*. Tonight was fabulous.

Twenty - Three

Trust Funds and No Funds

This place is going to be expensive I can already tell by the lobby. I didn't even think to ask Cabot what the rent cost before coming. I expected it to be within my price range, but I didn't really know her that well to assume. Turns out, she's a trust fund baby of her wealthy millionaire father from Connecticut who made all his money in stocks and selling software at a young age. She's the only child too, so that explains a few things.

"I hope you love it. I'm for real ready to move in if you are," Cabot says as she guides me towards the elevator.

A lot of buildings don't even have an elevator, so I know it's going to be pricey. Everything looks modern and new like they renovated the whole building. New York City isn't just popping up new buildings.

We get to the tenth floor, and a British guy in his early thirties who is dressed in a nicely tailored suit greets us. This is going to be super serious I can already tell. The dark hardwood floors and stainless steel appliances in the kitchen, the bathrooms with the walk in glass shower, the views of the city from the balcony. There's a master bedroom and a smaller guest room. This location is really good according to Cabot and the realtor. Isn't that what they all want you to think though?

"This looks amazing! I'm sure I can't afford it though. I can already guess just by looking at it."

"The rent is $3,760 a month, plus utilities. There is a rooftop with grills and abundant seating for parties. The views are incredible. You can see Staten Island from up there and the Highline," he chimes in his very cute accent. I have a thing for guys with accents, clearly.

"Wow, definitely out of my price range. What do you think, Cabot?"

"I think it is absolutely perfect-just what I need to get over my ex. Scarlett, I will take the master and pay the utilities. You should be able to afford it this way," she said as she took out her checkbook.

"I don't think I can let you do that. I will feel terrible. I should be able to afford it, though."

"Don't even think about it. You just started working, and I'm the one who asked you to move," she said reassuringly.

We sat down with the British man and signed the lease agreement. I'm so ready to move out of the Quinlan's I didn't even call my mom or dad to ask their opinion. Chase thought it was a good idea to have a coworker as a roommate that way we could vent to each other about our day. I didn't think it was a big deal, but I didn't even do a background check on Cabot like I usually do with people I just met. I just feel like I can trust her. Something about her being in distress and keeping her cool led me to believe she would be a good roommate. She's handling things so well with her breakup.

We are given the grand tour of the building, and I must say I am in love with the place. It's so much nicer than where Chase lives, but he does live over a restaurant. We can't move in for ten days because they have to run credit checks and backgrounds on us. They have to make sure they aren't letting Harry and Marv move into their very *swanky* apartment building. The realtor said they want to wait until the first of the month for us to move in to make things smoother on their end. I'm fine with waiting because it gives me time to find furniture to rent and I'll be paid by then.

I wonder how close this place is to Hugh and Chase- my boyfriends. I know it's probably far from Chase because he lives on the other side of town. Hugh lives on Madison Avenue, so it can't be very far from him.

After we're done with the tour, we decide to go out for celebratory cocktails as official roommates. Even though they have to run background checks, the guy said we have it in the bag. I'm sure Cabot slipped him a Benjamin to make it happen. I wouldn't put it past her. I didn't realize how wealthy she was, but she wasn't too shy about it. She seemed very open about her money, but not bitchy. I guess when you're trying to acquire an apartment in the city you put all your cards on the table, so they know you mean business.

"So when are you going to tell me more about yourself?!" Cabot asks after the cheers to our new place over a couple glasses of vino.

I wasn't really sure what I should tell her. I don't want to lie and start our friendship out like that, but I can't tell her the whole truth.

"There's not much to know! I grew up in Charleston, South Carolina. I love to draw, but I should say I'm more into doodling. I'm not very good at art, but I enjoy it and in my free time. It helps with my stress levels. I am currently seeing two promising guys right now that have me totally consumed and overwhelmed at the same time. I have a segment due in two weeks on how to get a holiday hook-up. I'm not excited about it by the way. Maybe you can help. I have a sister that's seven years younger, and my parents are divorced. I'm not wealthy, but my grandparents are very well off and well known in town. If I have a trust fund, I don't know about it yet."

I'm being honest; I didn't mention going to college in New York.

"You sound fascinating Scarlett Hanes. I think we will be fast friends. I like to have fun, and it seems like you do too. Let's just let our hair down and do the damn thing," she said as she literally took her hair down from her very tight sock bun.

"Sounds good to me; you sound very interesting as well, Cabot Vanderbilt. I wear my hair down a lot, *metaphorically* and *literally*."

We closed our tabs and went our separate ways. Cabot was staying with her cousin, Carmen on the Lower East Side until she moved in with me. I can't imagine going through what she has with her ex-fiancé. I'm hoping I'm never in that predicament. I got back to the Quinlan's and rushed upstairs to take a shower. I'm so ready for bed and to put some comfortable clothes on. I'm not sure how or when I should tell Lisa and Donald about my new place, but it's inevitable. I'm not sure if the whole thing will fall through or not. I want to wait until the background checks come back clean before I let them know. I hate for them to have it in their mind when I was moving out and then have to tell them I need to stay a little longer. I will just wait a few days and hope they receive the news gracefully. All I know is that I am so glad tomorrow starts the weekend.

Twenty - Four

Cat Out of the Bag

Friday has become my favorite day of the week. I'm sure I'm not alone here. I like Saturday and Sunday, but there is something about the anticipation of the weekend. I love knowing I don't have to work for two days. Cabot had to cancel her hair appointment last minute so luckily I just took it for her. I needed some fresh highlights and a trim, so I figured now is as good as any time. Hopefully, it won't cost an arm and a leg because I don't have *giraffe* money like she does. My grandfather always said people who have boatloads of money and spend it frivolously have "giraffe" money. I still don't know why it has to be a giraffe, but it stuck so I say it now.

I also want to go shopping tomorrow before my date because I need some new clothes to go out in. I have so many work clothes but not so many date clothes. I like to get a new outfit when I have something I'm really looking forward to.

I didn't think I would get a text until tomorrow, but Hugh decided to be romantic apparently.

"Hope you're excited, I have a lovely evening planned for us, Ms. Hanes."

I really like how he refers to me like that. Perhaps it will be *Mrs.* soon. I can't believe I'm going to this much trouble to look good for a date, but this is special. I've been anticipating our next date since he took me out for drinks. I haven't talked to Chase much over the course of the week because he had a deadline to meet and he was going home for a long weekend. I was actually relieved that he wouldn't be in town while I'm with Hugh. It allowed me to focus on Hugh and not get clouded like I did with Chase at his house.

I love getting my hair done especially at a new salon where I don't know anyone. I feel like I can totally open up to the stylist and tell them all about my life. It's like I pay them a large amount of money to listen to me, much like a therapist, and an added perk, they make me look pretty. I don't even care how much it cost at this point I'm just excited to be getting pampered for the first time in months.

The workday is now over, and my appointment is for 5:45 in midtown. I mapped it out, and I can actually walk from here if I want. I don't want to so I hail a cab. It's liberating not taking the subway everywhere I went. I feel in charge of my life when I hail a cab.

After the quick ten-minute ride, I hop out and grab a snack at a corner deli. I'm not sure how long this appointment will last, so I wanted to eat something beforehand. Cabot let me know they serve wine and champagne during the appointment. I definitely want to eat before I'm too buzzed to remember food is necessary. I didn't have any plans tonight but to get my hair done and be low-key. It sucks to have my hair look all pretty for nothing, but at least I'll be well rested for tomorrow, and my hair will probably still look good.

I walk into the salon and feel a bit out of place. I've been to nice hair salons before, but I usually knew someone there that was getting their hair done. Obviously, I don't' really know anyone in the city, so this is a bit awkward. I'm pretty sure this kind of salon has regulars, and they know I'm not one of them. The receptionist greeted me and asked if I wanted anything to drink. I didn't want to be a burden after feeling like I was intruding, so I just said white wine to keep things basic. Obviously, I'm more of a champagne girl but perhaps halfway through if things are going well I'll feel bold enough to switch it up.

I notice a lot of girls my age or Cabot's are in the salon. I don't see anyone middle-aged or older. I guess this is a salon for young women in their twenties. I'm not worried about it though because I'm not trying to make friends at a hair salon.

The stylist, named Jen, who was going to hopefully help my root situation, finally called me back; she seemed friendly. She has an interesting look; she was very petite and had a short pixie haircut with bright red hair. She reminds me of Tinkerbelle or something in a cartoon. I always feel a little tense before getting my hair done because everyone always wants to do outlandish things with it. I never like to color outside the lines too much with my hair because it's my security blanket.

Jen asks me how I want to do my hair, and we get started. I notice almost every chair is filled with a client, and it made me feel good knowing this place must be reputable. I start to talk to Jen and feel comfortable opening up as she foiled my highlights. She asks me about my job and whom I'm dating. I tell her about Chase and Hugh. I even told her about Donald and how he treated me and how he gave me the watch from Cartier. I let her know I was in a bit of a love triangle, but she said if I was going to this much trouble to look good for a man he must be something special. I gave her the full details of how we met and how he has an amazing Australian accent.

The girl next to me is overly curious and seems to be listening in on my conversation with Jen. I want to tell her to mind her own business, but she became busy texting away on her phone after I stopped talking about my relationships. I feel a little drunk after drinking almost four glasses of Sonoma Cutrer; the best wine I've ever had. I lost track of time completely. I may have slipped about how I got my job at Cosmo...

After Jen shampooed my hair and cut it, I absolutely loved the way she styled it. I'm not used to layers, but she made me look sophisticated. I've always had really long, heavy hair, and she took it up a few inches. I'm not sure I was ready to part with that much hair, but nothing bothered me after drinking nearly a bottle of that delicious chardonnay.

I walk to the counter to check out, and she tells me it will cost $280. I can't believe what I'm hearing. How the hell can someone afford to do this every couple of months? I decide it was ok to splurge this one time, but I will be finding someone more affordable after this. Plus, I probably shouldn't develop a relationship with a stylist that now knows my secret.

I get home, and Lisa left a note on my door saying she is once again out with one of her girlfriends leaving me, and Donald stuck on a Friday night with the baby. I guess it won't be so bad since we've done this before and I know what to expect. I'm feeling good because my hair looks awesome, I have a whole new look, and I'm buzzing like crazy.

"Wow! Your hair looks great!" Donald exclaims, still wearing his work attire and drinking a small glass of what looked to be scotch.

"Thanks, I went to this fancy salon called, Kiwa, they charge a ton but I think it was worth it this one time."

"I would have to agree. I actually have something for you. I know you're getting anxious about your date tomorrow, so I got you these to make you look extra beautiful," he says as he slides the small blue box towards me.

"Tiffany's? Are you *fucking* kidding me," I said by accident. Whoops!

"Just open it. It's nothing."

"Diamond earrings? Donald. Are you serious right now? This is not just *nothing*. What would your wife say?!"

I'm not even hearing what I'm saying. I have no filter when I'm drunk, so it just came out.

"My wife doesn't have to know about it. She is out with her personal trainer drinking and being a slut. She doesn't care about me the way you do."

"I thought she was out with a girlfriend? That's what she told me at least. I'm sorry she doesn't care. What do you mean the way I do?"

"You are just so sweet to me. You are deserving of something so beautiful."

"Thank you, but I can't accept these."

"Of course, you can. Just don't tell Lisa. I didn't tell her about the watch, and I won't tell her about these earrings either. Just like she doesn't tell me what she does when she's out with her trainer. I have my own personal bank account she doesn't know about. We are in a difficult place right now."

"I was under the impression things were going so well between you two…the other night when you went out on your date, you seemed really happy."

"Key word: seemed. We were just hammered. We argued at dinner and all the way home. We were just drunk and frustrated, so we turned it into a sexual rage that we both regret."

I can't believe I have brand new earrings from Tiffany's. I've never owned jewelry like this and I really don't want to give them back. I know I should, but he told me not to. Much like the watch situation, I feel guilty, but I can't return something he insists on me having. They are *really* beautiful and something that I could wear every day. He probably wants me to give him something in return, but I simply could never come between someone's marriage the way Naomi did with my family. I will never be a home wrecker.

We end up playing cards in the living room and enjoy some more vino. As if I hadn't had enough tonight I decide to drink more. I feel like my life is a shipwreck. I don't even know how to explain it but when I said it out loud to Jen I felt like I was in serious need of change. I want to live away from these people, date one guy at a time, and be normal. I like Donald, and I like Lisa, but I can't see myself doing this much longer, or I'll end up with a Range Rover.

I'm really excited about moving in with Cabot, to have a girl to do things with instead of a middle aged *married* man every Friday night.

Twenty - Five

Hey BTW-I'm Kind of Married

Today was going to be a good day no matter what. I'm not going to let anything stand in the way of my happiness. I want to feel good and look good for Hugh tonight. I feel like I've been preparing for my senior prom the past twenty-four hours getting ready for this date. Sometimes it requires a little extra something to feel your best. My mom would totally agree that going the distance to make an impression is important. Not sure if she would say it's worth $280 and a new outfit on top of that but she's not here to judge or tell me what I can or can't do.

I decide not to set an alarm because I have nothing to do today besides shopping, and I need to recover from all the alcohol I consumed last night. I woke up with my face looking super swollen and my head pounding. A hot shower and some green juice should do the trick. I don't really like these juice cleanses, but they certainly make me feel and look better. I quickly get ready because it's already noon and I want to get home by three so I can have enough time to get ready for my *prom*.

Donald is arguing with Lisa in the kitchen, so I just grab the drink out of the fridge and tell them I will see them later. I'm not even sure they hear me because I say it so fast to avoid getting in the middle of whatever confrontation they are dealing with. I hope that Lisa hasn't discovered the jewelry. I might need to stay the night at Hugh's whether I like it or not. Who am I kidding? That is most definitely going to happen if I have it my way.

I only went in five shops when I finally find the perfect little black dress that I'm going to wear tonight. It's really hard to find anything sexy that is long sleeved, so I was shopping longer than I expected. By the time I got lunch, shopped around, and got home it was already 4:30. I'm way past my time allotment, but I figured he wasn't coming to get me until seven tonight. I can't believe I'm letting him know where I've been living, but I'll be able to tell him I'm moving out really soon so it won't matter much.

Once I get home, I place my outfit on a hanger and pulled out the tall black boots I'm going to wear with it. I feel like this is sexy enough with my new hair, my makeup, and my new jewelry. I like to keep things fairly simple and not go overboard. I want him to think I got ready really effortlessly. I shave my legs and everything else necessary for the evening and get ready. I put my music on and jam out while doing my makeup. I'm getting really anxious, and then my mom calls me to FaceTime.

"Honey, you look so pretty where are you going?"

"I'm going on a date with Hugh. He has a *lovely* evening planned for us, so he says."

"How fun. Make sure you use protection. With a guy that hot he's probably been around the block a time or two if you know what I mean," she winked awkwardly.

"Eww, stop mom. I'm going to pretend you didn't just advise me to have him wear a condom tonight and move on. What's new with you?"

"I'm calling you to tell you that I booked my flight to come for Thanksgiving. I hope that's ok with you. I didn't book a hotel yet but I can if I need to."

"You will be able to stay with me in my new apartment by then. I think we are supposed to move in by the end of the month."

"That's wonderful honey. I can't wait to see it. I will spend most of the night looking up furniture rental companies or see if I can find a good deal on it from IKEA or something. I don't want you to stress over it. I will help you."

"Thanks, mom, I love you. I have to go now. He's coming to get me in thirty minutes," I say as I apply another coat of mascara.

It's good to hear from my mom, but SO weird that she's visualizing me having sex later. I have never talked like that with her, but I guess she was right. It's best to be safe when it comes to the first time with a guy you aren't even really serious with. I don't view Hugh as the type of guy that sleeps around with a lot of women. Once I find out how things with Emma went, I will gauge the situation and take control.

I'm going to throw up because Hugh is supposed to be here in nearly five minutes, and I'm not ready yet. I want to pack a few things in my purse in case I end up staying the night. I decide to throw a pair of panties in the zipper portion of my bag and a toothbrush. I must be feeling really confident because if things don't go as I'm hoping, I'm going to feel like a total moron. I have to stay calm or things will feel really strange. When we went out for drinks, I thought he was just being friendly. Now I know that he potentially wants to date me, so things are different.

I hear a knock on the front door and realize it's either a pizza being delivered or it's my date. It's Hugh holding one single pink rose and Lisa answers before I have the chance. She calls me down, and I overhear her flirting with Hugh telling him how handsome he is and how she loves his accent. That must get old.

"I'm coming, be right there," I shouted from the top of the stairs.

I apply my lip-gloss one last time before coming down. I truly feel like I'm going to some high school dance or something. I feel a bit ridiculous dressing up so much but from what I could see walking down the stairs he is dressed nicely. He has on dark jeans with a white button down and a black blazer. I hadn't seen him dressed this nice at work, so it's surprising. He looks really sophisticated, and I love it. Nice to know he can wear many hats…

"Hello beautiful, you look stunning tonight, I love your new hair," he said while handing me the long stem pink rose. It's sort of charming and weird at the same time. Must be something men do in his country. None of the guys I've ever dated showed up holding a single rose. I now feel like I'm on the Bachelorette…and I *will* accept this rose.

"Likewise, and thank you," I said as I handed Lisa the rose and shut the door.

She gave me a big grin and thumbs up as I left. Apparently she approves of Hugh.

"I know you liked the car service last time, so I got it again for us. I wanted to make tonight special for you."

"You're doing a good job thus far," I said as I stepped into the car.

"You didn't tell me you were living with a married couple. They seem really nice from what I could infer."

"Yea, I guess I left that bit of information out. I didn't want you to think it was strange. They are just family friends. They have a really nice house, and it's been comfortable for me. I was living at home until I got this job. I was sure I would end up here I just didn't know when."

"I think that's neat that they are letting you stay, Lisa was very friendly."

"I can only imagine why. But I won't be with them too much longer. Cabot Vanderbilt and I signed a lease to move into a new apartment in a week and a half. I'm excited."

"I don't know her, but I'm sure you're excited to get a new place of your own. Hopefully, you'll invite me over to see it when you move in."

Things are going really well. Hugh is being *super* romantic and his crazy ex-hook up Emma, whatever she was, semantics, has not been brought up yet. I'm trying to avoid talking about relationships or anything serious. I want to seem like it doesn't bother me but also make sure he knows I am not going to compete with anyone else for his affection. I have no idea where we are going, but I imagine it to be something wonderful and exotic.

"I know I promised to take you out, but I decided to do something a little more intimate," he said as he grabbed my hand to place in his.

"Where are you taking me?"

"You'll see..."

I don't know where he lives yet so it's a mystery as to where we will end up. The drive didn't take very long, but we finally ended up at a very tall building; a building that I recognized as soon as the car pulled over. This is MY new apartment building. This is where I'm going to move in with Cabot.

"Wait...do you live here?" I say with my jaw practically dropped to the floor.

"I sure do. I moved in this summer when it opened. It's really nice here I think you'll like it."

"I know I like it because this is the building I'm moving into with Cabot!"

"What! That is a wild coincidence. What floor will you two live on?"

"We will be on the 10th floor. Where are you?"

"I'm on the penthouse level; so not too far from you. I'm excited we'll be neighbors soon," he said as we walked to the elevator.

"Ditto!"

We arrive at the penthouse level after a short ride up the elevator, no making out yet of course. I definitely want him to make a move, but I will just let things happen naturally. I kind of wish I hadn't got so gussied up for a date at his house. Waste of a perfectly good outfit. It has me a bit disappointed, to be honest.

"Ok, I know it seems crazy not going out but I thought you would like the views from the rooftop, and I've cooked us something delicious," he said as we walked into the door of his "penthouse."

"Your place is huge! The views up here are quite impressive, Mr. Hamilton."

"Yes, they are. That is why I chose the place. What's the point of living in the city if you can't have a good view? I just need to grab these filets and we can head up to the roof. You told me you like rooftops last week so I thought this would make you happy. Plus I cook a mean filet and potatoes."

"Can't wait," I say as I stare at every facet of this penthouse.

I sat on the barstool at his island waiting for him to get everything for our meal. I wasn't expecting a cooked meal from Hugh at all. He's too beautiful to be a good cook on top of it all. It's very possible it won't be good though so I will wait and see. His apartment is nearly 1,800 square feet if I had to guess. Very modern and well lit. He has really nice leather furniture and beautiful lamps and cool oriental rugs. His place is much more sophisticated than Chase's. That was to be expected, though. I can see myself here in the near future; having many sleep over's once I move in my place. I still can't believe we will be working together and living in the same building. What are the odds?

We finally went to the rooftop, and I saw the beautiful white lights set up and the table with another rose in a vase, this one is white, and candles all around. There's a bottle of Veuve Chicquot champagne on the table in a marble wine chiller that happily going to be consumed by me. This is the most romantic setting I have ever had for a date. I can't believe he went to so much trouble on my behalf. I really feel like he likes me now. This is the kind of setting you only see on unrealistic romance movies when a guy is about to propose. I feel like Kate in the movie Kate & Leopold when he does a very similar evening for her towards the end of the movie. All we are missing is the violinist, which I'm totally ok with not being here.

"This is beautiful; I'm so happy to be here with you. Despite the cold I can honestly say this is perfect."

"If you're cold I can run down and get you a blanket. It's not a problem; I'll be right back."

"Thanks, that's really sweet. I have thin southern blood, remember?"

Hugh leaves to go downstairs and decides to keep his cell phone facing *up* on the table. Instincts tell me to go through it, but I know I shouldn't. It's staring right at me. Instead of having to go through it, a text pops up on the locked screen. I guess he didn't turn the feature off where you can read the text while it's locked. It's from Emma-of course.

"I'm not signing these papers!!!! You can forget about it. You're the one who wants this, not me."

I try very hard not to assume what this could mean, but context clues lead me to believe Emma is asking for a *divorce*. It certainly doesn't sit well with me because I don't want to bring it up or he will know I read his text. I want to avoid anything like this at all cost tonight. I'm going to get drunk and pretend I didn't see that very cryptic message.

"Here's a sweatshirt, and a blanket. I think we should pop this champagne and put on the real coat, what do you say?"

"Yes. Absolutely, thanks. I think your phone went off by the way. I heard it chime a couple minutes ago."

I tried to say it all nonchalant hoping to see what his reaction will be to her text. He picks up his phone and looks very perturbed. I want to ask what it's about, but I don't want to pry. I'm just hoping it doesn't kill the mood.

"I'm going throw these steaks on, you must be starving," he said as he walked towards the grill area. I can't help but notice he seems a bit disheveled after reading Emma's text.

"I am. Is everything ok?"

"It will be; soon."

I'm starting to wonder if I'm on a date with a married man. How could it be that he would keep something like this from me? I can't feel good about tonight knowing he is possibly going to cheat on his wife. I'm starting to get a knot in my stomach because I knew this was too good to be true.

We ate our dinner and didn't say very much. I think Hugh is trying to avoid telling me the inevitable. He probably knows that I saw the text. In a way, I didn't really care. He's an older guy, and he probably has a past. Everyone has a past. I feel like a hypocrite for even getting mad at him when he doesn't even know everything about me. I told him almost everything except the truth about where I went to college. It seemed pretty minuscule compared to lying about marital status.

"I think we should go inside and get warm. I'm thinking we can have some coffee and Irish cream to heat things up a bit. I'll even turn the fireplace on, and we can get more comfortable."

"That sounds like a good plan to me."

We cleaned up from dinner, and walked to the elevator. Hugh is being awfully quiet and I don't know what to say to break the ice. We get back inside and put the dishes in the sink. He pulls a bottle of Bailey's out, and started the coffee. He also pulled out some whipped cream and placed it on the counter.

"Wonder if we will put that whipped cream to good use later..." I ask trying to lighten the air in the room because right now you could cut the tension with a knife.

"How about we put it to good use now..."

"Perfect!"

The penthouse is much warmer than the roof, especially now that we are chasing each other around the kitchen with a bottle of whipped cream. It's a much better vibe than earlier when we were eating dinner. I knew that if he wanted to explain things, he would later. I'm really starting to feel the champagne and coffee kick in. I have whipped cream all over my face, and I don't want to get it on my new dress or in my hair, so I suggested we go to his bedroom.

"Why don't I help you slip out of that number, so you don't get it dirty," he says as he unzips the back, *slowly*.

"That sounds like a good idea, I wouldn't want to get dirty or anything-might have to shower off."

Hugh starts to kiss down the nape of my neck, slowly, going down to my lower back, kissing every inch of my body until he reaches my black lace thong that I got earlier to wear specifically for this very occasion. He slid them off carefully, and they hit the floor without a sound.

"Don't stop," I say as I start to kiss his neck and his lips.

Now on his king size bed, he unbuttons his shirt and throws it on the chair by the window. His body is *flawless* just as I imagined it to be. He unzips his pants, and I suggest that he let me do it instead.

"Keep going," he says as he kisses down my stomach into my lower regions.

I feel so comfortable with him for whatever reason. He knew exactly what to do to please me. As I start to moan, I feel a tingling sensation that I didn't want to end. He took my bra off with one hand and tossed it on the chair with his shirt. All of New York City is probably looking in on us right now because his room has a huge window with a view of the city. I don't even care. Something about everyone watching was turning me on all of a sudden.

"Nothing about this feels wrong," I say as I slide his briefs off and throw them across the room landing on the flat screen that's mounted on the wall.

We are both completely naked now and about to have sex. I can't believe I'm actually doing this knowing he could be possibly married. Those papers are probably divorce papers she was referring to. I can handle that. I can be ok with the fact that he has been married before. I can be ok with the fact he left that very important detail out of the twenty-one questions we played on our first date…

I didn't expect it to be so bright in here when we woke up I was practically blinded. It's six in the morning, and Hugh is sound asleep. I didn't realize I had passed out. I guess we had too much fun. I can't believe I just had sex with Hugh. It was so incredible, though. It's the best sex I've *ever* had. I'm shocked that I stayed the night, but I guess I wanted this to happen.

"Good morning, handsome," I say to him softly as I wrap my arms around him.

"Good morning my love," he says to me as he turns around to face me.

"Well, what a night."

"Yes, I do think it was fun, Scarlett."

"What's wrong? You seem upset," I say in a lowered voice as I sat up.

"I have to tell you something. I feel incredibly guilty not telling you from the beginning, but if I had, you wouldn't like me anymore."

I'm thinking that I know what he's about to say. I feel like I'm in no position to get mad at him considering I haven't been fair to him either. I' d been keeping a secret from him as well. I just can't seem to divulge that kind of information yet.

"Yes? What is it? You're scaring me!"

"I'm *kind* of married. But I promise we are getting a divorce."

Twenty-Six

Shell Shock

"What the HELL did you just say?"

I can't believe my ears. I don't know why I acted so surprised, though. I read the text from Emma and assumed he was. I was hoping it was some legal matter over property or a dog or something. I didn't expect him to be full on married.

"I know this may be shocking, but I am indeed married. We are separated and have been for a year now. That's why I told you things weren't that serious with Emma, and I was dating other women."

"Not that serious? It's serious. Serious as a heart attack," I say with a panicked voice.

"I know you must think I'm a terrible person, but I really like you. I signed the divorce papers the day I met you at the airport. I was on the way to have the papers filed in Atlanta where we got married, and Emma refused to sign them. She's the one who cheated on me, and she's been trying to make things right ever since."

"I guess I understand. What I don't understand is why you feel you couldn't tell me?"

"I just didn't want to shock you. I've told the past few girls I've dated, and they freak out and never speak to me again. I didn't want to risk that with you. I like you way too much. I was only married to her for eight months. I tried to have it annulled, but we had been married too long by that point."

"Eight months isn't very long. I'm going to have to process this. I feel kind of weird knowing I slept with a married man last night…one who I really, really like."

"I understand. Take all the time you need. I want you to know that I'm going to get those papers signed hell or high water, and I will be exclusive with you once they are. I really like you, Ms. Hanes," he says as he touches my face and pulls me in for a kiss.

I can't resist him. I can't even imagine why anyone in their right mind would cheat on a guy like Hugh. He is so amazing in every way; except the fact that he flat out lied and was deceptive with me. I have to keep in mind that I'm doing the same thing.

I gathered my things and left wearing a New York Yankees sweatshirt and some gray sweatpants he let me borrow. Talk about the *walk of shame*. I think it's safe to say that I have great material for my segment due next week. Thankfully, I had some clean underwear so I didn't feel like a complete trash bucket. I want to be mad with Hugh but I really can't. He put his heart on the line telling me about his marriage and divorce. I just wonder if we would've slept together had he told me initially after he read his text. My guess is he would have taken this to the grave if he could have.

He's making me an acai "smoothie bowl" or whatever while I get ready and I figure I might as well eat it so I can save money on breakfast. I'm not mad at him I just feel *super* weird knowing he is married. I'm not sure if I want this kind of baggage to start a relationship. Especially since it's possible, I will be running into Emma at work now. I try to eat as fast as I can without eating like a complete savage.

"Scarlett, please don't be upset with me. I'm *really very* sorry I didn't tell you before, but it's embarrassing having a marriage that only lasted as long as it did. Emma is a crazy jealous girl, and she would do anything to get me to love her again. It's just not going to happen. She made it to where I can't trust her anymore. I hope you will forgive me and still give me a chance," he said with a cute smirk on his face.

It's hard to stay mad at him when he is so freaking sexy; standing in the kitchen with his hair all tousled and only wearing gym shorts.

"I understand. I'm not mad at you. I just want to make sure she signs those papers before I sleep with a married man again. I feel wrong doing it this way," I said as I finish my very delicious breakfast.

"Trust me. Those papers will be signed because I can't resist being with you too long. Until then, I will wine and dine you and keep things PG-13, I promise."

"Deal."

I feel like I need to take a very long, hot, shower and think about what just happened. I decide to take the subway home even though he offered to pay for my cab. I don't feel like any special treatment the way I'm dressed. I just feel kind of *stupid*. I'm not really the type of girl to just have sex with a guy after knowing him for only a couple of months. I feel like calling my mom to tell her, but I think she would forbid me to see him again. I instead put on my headphones and tune out the thoughts going through my mind.

I get back to notice that the car isn't out front, and the Quinlan's are not here. I'm actually super happy that they are gone because I want to shower and go to sleep. I'm sad even though I was so happy last night. I guess nothing is perfect, but it really did feel that way for a while. I've held Hugh to such a high standard since I met him at the airport. I just knew he would be the perfect gentleman that I wouldn't be able to date because he was surely taken; I wasn't wrong, he is most definitely taken.

In a way, the lure of dating him isn't so alluring anymore. I want to feel the same, but something has changed. I've sobered up and come to my senses. I can't see him again until the papers are signed. I know that I said I could see him, but I really don't want to. It just doesn't feel right.

I finally wake up around three that afternoon feeling like a bus hit me. I still had all my clothes from last night strung out on the floor and the clothes Hugh let me borrow to wear home. Everything is a mess. I really need someone to help me get out of this nightmare. I check my phone to have messages from Hugh, Chase, and Lisa and my sister.

"Hey, how's your weekend going? It's raining here, and I miss talking to you." –Chase

"I hope you won't stay away too long. I had a lot of fun last night, and I can't stop thinking about you." –Hugh

"Hey, Scarlett, we decided to take a little trip to New Jersey to see my relatives. We should be back tomorrow morning really early. Help yourself to whatever is in the fridge!" –Lisa

"Hey, sis how's life up there? Its seventy-seven degrees here and we're going out on grandfather's boat. Miss you!" -Savannah

Don't even feel like responding to any of them so I throw my phone on the floor and go back to sleep. I don't want to face anyone right now. I just want to pretend that Hugh is still the sexy man that I am totally smitten with; Chase is too nice, and I don't deserve him. I probably just need to tell him I can't see him like I did last week anymore. There's something to be said about being single in the city. Maybe I need to uncomplicate things for a while. Just when I think that's a good idea, I realize that I'm going to be living in the same building as Hugh.

A night in by myself doesn't sound terrible. I'll have free reign over

the TV, and I can eat whatever I want without anyone around to judge me. I thought about calling Cabot to come over, but I realized it was Sunday, and we both have to be at work bright and early. I need to lay off the alcohol for a while because it seems nothing good happens after I drink. I will enjoy a nice Ryan Gosling chick flick and eat something with high caloric value. There's nothing wrong with that combination.

I order Chinese take-out because there is nothing but vegetables in the fridge and breast milk in the freezer. I'm not that desperate. I don't think I should feel so bad for myself considering I'm not the one who screwed up this time. I'm not saying Hugh screwed up, but he did kind of mess up how I feel about him. He is seriously going to have to fix this before I let him back into my good graces again.

Texting Chase back is probably a mistake, but I do it because I'm lonely and bored here by myself. He's a good friend if nothing else and he's easy to talk to. I really want to tell him about Hugh being married, but it would upset him I think. No guy wants to hear about your date with another man. That would be like throwing a drink in his face after how things went between us at his house last week. I keep things light and ask him how his trip went. He isn't really flirting, so I'm relieved. I just need some normalcy for *one* day. I can't imagine how it will be this week when I run into Hugh. Guess I will be avoiding the caffeine at all cost. Sounds like a blast.

Twenty - Seven

Just call me Carrie Bradshaw

The next few days I focused on writing my segment for the December issue trying not to think about Hugh or Chase or anyone for that matter. I need to go to a coffee shop or check into a nice hotel like Carrie did often on Sex & the City so I can get this done. Problem is, Hugh has turned into my version of Mr. Big and Chase is Aiden. Such a predicament having two amazing men after me-haha.

I don't really have anything I can write about except my own experiences. I didn't want to get Hugh in trouble, but I need to tell my story because it is a story worth sharing. I can just change the names and change the scene a little. He won't be mad because I'll tell him I have to write this segment and I got so distracted by our little escapade that he owes me. I figure I can use my experience with Chase as well. Maybe neither of these guys will even read my article, and it will be a non-issue.

I skipped coffee every day this week until now because I am absolutely dying trying to finish this piece. I've worked so hard to change things up and write the perfect column that I haven't even taken a lunch break once this week.

My segment is due at five today when the workday is over, and I'm supposed to go by the apartment with Cabot to start moving some things in. I ordered some furniture, and I'm having it all delivered tonight. Courtney already emailed me this morning reminding me that she needed my segment "ON TIME!" I'm sure I can finish this, but I need to talk to Hugh first to run it by him. I wouldn't feel right publishing this without his consent. I met him in the coffee-room at his usual time, and we talked it out.

"Hey, beautiful, haven't seen you in a while. What are you up to?" Hugh asked in a normal way like it's no big deal.

"I've been really busy writing this segment for Macy since she's out sick. Courtney really demanded I have it done by five today, and I've been procrastinating because I need your blessing before I write it."

I explain the situation and tell him that I promise I won't involve anyone's names and surprisingly he doesn't mind. I'm shocked, but I guess he really feels bad for the way things went down. He actually agreed it would make for an interesting piece.

It was really good to see him. I suddenly felt my heart race a little faster. I don't want anyone here knowing who I date I don't think it's professional, and I really don't think it's any of their business. Hugh says he spoke with Emma, and she's agreed to sign the papers next week when she comes to the city for work. I guess that meant it's possible I would run into them since I'll be living at my new place by then.

My segment is churning out rather quickly. I decided to go to my buddy Cooper to let him read it first and see what he thinks before I turn it into Courtney. After all, he was with me when she demanded I write this heinous crap. I feel like he's someone who could read this with an unbiased opinion perhaps in part because he's gay.

To my surprise, he reads it and laughs out loud during a few parts of my story and finishes it with a huge smile on his face.

"Scarlett, this is *brilliant*. So fresh and fun! I like how you spun this disastrous holiday hook up into something fun. The readers will love it."

Great. He thinks my life is a *disaster*. Hopefully, nobody will realize this is written from personal experience. I know it's a bit of a disaster, but I'm not sure I was willing to admit it to myself.

"Great! I'm so glad you like it. I hope Courtney will. I have to go do some last minute editing, and I think I'll be ready to turn it in."

I have a slight sickness in my stomach. I really want to be ok with this, but I'm not. The whole world will be reading this story they think is about some poor girl that "got had." I don't have time to fix it now I just have to hope that Emma doesn't put the pieces of the puzzle together when and if she reads it.

I add a few made up stories within the segment to make it seem more realistic, but the biggest story is the one where the girl sleeps with a married man by accident. I'm sure the readers will eat this up. Surely people still seek pleasure from other's mishaps. I used to read these magazines in high school and think so many people had screwed up relationships. I never actually imagined that I would be writing for one of those magazines and sharing my actual experiences with the world.

It's now four in the afternoon, and I decide to turn my piece in early in case the computer shut down or something. I didn't expect a reaction out of Courtney so fast but apparently she read it right away.

Scarlett,

I don't normally say this, but your piece is downright <u>brilliant</u>. I love it. We might have to talk about switching your focus here pretty soon from fashion to relationships. Well done.

Courtney

I'm surprised with her response. I want to be upset, but I'm over the moon right now. I'm like a runner with a high after a marathon. I'm so happy that I can check this off my to-do list. This could have totally backfired. Courtney could have hated it, but I'm so glad she doesn't. I hate how things went down between Hugh and I, but it turns out that everything happens for a reason.

I decide I should text Hugh that Courtney liked my piece considering he is the reason behind the madness. He's my muse for this piece.

"I'm glad I could help. I hope this means I'm back in your good graces," Hugh chimes in his text.

"Yes, I would say you have earned it."

"Please tell me that means you'll come over later?"

"I'll be moving furniture into my apartment tonight. I guess I could stop by since you aren't too far out of the way…"

"Can't wait."

I knew it couldn't last too long between us not seeing each other. I want to tell him everything about me, but I need to wait for the right time. I don't know if it's something I'll ever feel ok telling him, but I know I need to. It's not like I'm a serial killer. It's just very immature how I got my job and I don't want him to see me that way. He was really brave to tell me about his divorce and I'll try to be brave about my resume. I think I can hold off for a little longer…

Twenty - Eight

Unit 1005

Tonight brought back memories of when Addison and I moved into our freshman dorm room. I'm ready to start this new chapter in my life with Cabot; I hope I'm making the right decision. She's a bit pretentious and bratty sometimes, but I like her moxie. She keeps me on my toes, and I never feel bored around her. We get to start moving things in tonight even though our move in date is actually Saturday. Being that Hugh lives in the penthouse, and he has become friends with the manager, he asked this favor on behalf of his, "girlfriend" as he called me earlier. It had a nice ring to it I must say.

I told Lisa and Donald I was moving out last night over dinner. Surprisingly they both took it really well. I felt like Donald was sad but he kindly offered his help on Saturday with the heavy lifting. Luckily Cabot bought most of the furnishings for the apartment, and all I needed to buy was our TV and my room décor. My mom offered to help with this and let it be my Christmas gift. I just hope that things between Cabot and me work out, or I will be moving up to the penthouse.

I want things to look perfect for when my mom comes in a few weeks for Thanksgiving. Cabot showed me some of the furniture and kitchen items she ordered online the other day at work. She insisted on getting the Kate Spade *fine china* for our dishes and I wasn't going to stop her. At least when my mom comes she will have a nice place to stay. Maybe I will even introduce her to my *sexy* Australian boyfriend who lives upstairs. I can't believe I'm even referring to him as my boyfriend. It does feel better for the next time I decide to sleep with him knowing we aren't just a *fling*.

Cabot has her movers bringing up the furniture tonight for her room and the living room. She said that the kitchen should be fully stocked by Sunday. I only have my room stuff coming. We can go together to get a TV and all the other essentials we might need for our place. I can't believe how much it cost for my mom to have these movers bring in a bed, a nightstand, a dresser, and a headboard. Living in New York City is somewhat of a grind. We don't have washer and dryer hookups, but there's a laundry room in the basement of our building. Hugh actually has a washer and dryer in his penthouse that I planned on using as much as he'd let me. I'm sure after how things went down on our date last week that he'd even do it for me. Probably fold and iron everything too.

I'm tired of watching these men place things all strategically, so I decide to go see Hugh for a little while. Chances of me sleeping over are really great at this point because I'm really tired and don't feel like going back to Gramercy this late. I have some clothes in my new closet thinking this might happen. I'm ready to be with Hugh in the way we deserve to be. I feel like I just left Chase in the dust but, I think he understands that what we had was just a casual thing. He was fairly mature when I told him that I was seeing someone exclusively. I don't think he even has time for a girlfriend, honestly.

"Hey, babe! How's the moving going? I just made some chai tea if you're interested in some," Hugh said as he hugged me and wrapped his arms around my head to kiss my forehead.

"I would most definitely enjoy some tea even though I've never had any chai tea before."

"You'll love it. I promise."

"Speaking of love, how did you get Emma to sign the papers? I can't see that being an easy task. I'm happy about it, though; really happy."

"Well, everything has a price and apparently she didn't want me that bad. She just wanted my money. But lucky for me, I have enough to make her happy and get rid of her in the process."

"I hope that didn't set you back too much. I feel bad if I'm the one who pushed you to come to that."

"Not at all. I'm so relieved it's over between us. I would have paid her triple had I known I could have gotten out sooner."

I'm so relieved that he is finally a free man. I want to jump up and down with excitement. I'm so happy that everything is coming together for us, and we can finally be a couple without her looming over our heads like a dark cloud. I'm finally feeling the way I did about him when we first met. For a while there I was certain I could get over him. Now, there's not a chance in hell. I'm falling for him. I'm falling fast.

The night went on, and Hugh, and I talked about my new apartment, unit 1005 down on the tenth floor. I probably wouldn't have moved in

with Cabot had I known my boyfriend would be living five floors above us; seems like a waste of money but my grandparents certainly would not approve of me living with Hugh before we were at least engaged. I don't want to get ahead of myself considering the man just got divorced.

"Hey, how does a hot bath sound to you?" Hugh says as he starts taking his shirt off and heads towards the bedroom.

"Sounds like a perfect way to end the night," I say as I take my shirt off as well.

We both just left our clothes on the floor of the kitchen and went into the master bathroom. I walk in, and he had the little candles lit from our first date around the bathtub. It's like he had this planned all night hoping I would stay over. He's quite the romantic if I must say.

"This looks amazing…you really know the way to my heart," I say as I slowly took off the rest of my clothes and slid into the hot bubble bath.

"Let me turn some music on and I will join you in a second."

How can this night get any better? I guess if he was actually in the bath with me. But really, how can my life be any better than it is at this very moment. I landed the guy of my dreams. I have an incredible job at the best company in the world. I have a great family and great friends. I want to go on the balcony and tell the entire city that I'm in a relationship with Hugh Hamilton.

"Get in here! Now!"

"I'm coming! I wanted to set the mood," he says as he throws the towel on the floor and gets in with me. I still can't get over how sexy he is-if you know what I mean. I'm lucky. I know that.

"You already did. Everything is great."

Twenty - Nine

The Choice

I'm finally starting to get into the groove of things at work. I feel like the planets are aligned perfectly right now. I feel like I can make it here in New York City. Having my mom here for Thanksgiving was perfect, and we had a great time touring the city, and she happened to love Hugh, so that is great. Hugh and I both are coming home for Christmas and New Years, and I can't wait to introduce him to everyone. Everything is *amazing*.

I don't normally check my phone until lunch but today is dragging because I don't have any segments due since it's almost Christmas and the December issue has already come out. My relationship segment with *my* name attached to it in *bold* is now in my apartment thanks to my very thoughtful roommate, Cabot who thought it was frame worthy. It's a constant reminder of how my relationship with Hugh started, but also a reminder that I'm better in the fashion world. Courtney really wants me to take Macy's spot, but I can't take her job. I told her I can substitute anytime, but I really do enjoy working with clothes, jewelry, and shoes. I also don't want to get that kind of reputation around the office that I steal people's jobs. I need to save face as much as possible around here.

I go onto all my various social media accounts and find myself on Facebook. I don't even really go on Facebook that much because it isn't really my preferred outlet for news. All I see on my feed is updates about someone's latest engagement or baby announcement. I guess people can still find you on here and stalk you to send messages. I go on to see this:

December 16, 2015

11:30 am

Scarlett,

I didn't think it was you until I saw you on a local news station here in Atlanta. Apparently you saved a man's life on the beach, and the guy is dead now. The story is describing you as the young woman from College of Charleston. "The heroin that saved a man's life." I was under the impression you went to Columbia. That's what Hugh told me… I wonder how your office would feel if they saw this little video I saved to my desktop…

If you want to keep your precious job at Cosmo you have two options: break up with Hugh and keep your job. Don't break up with Hugh and I'll go to your boss and tell her everything I know and show the video. Perhaps I'll just tell them anyways. Who knows…

I'll give you until Friday to figure this out. I'll know if you two broke up or not because I'm coming to the city this weekend for a shoot and I plan on having a conversation with Hugh. Maybe by then he'll know you're a liar.

-Emma *Hamilton*

What the hell? What am I supposed to do?! Why would someone come after me like this? Hugh did say she's bat shit crazy, so I can only imagine why she would do this, but now I'm screwed. I feel like my world just came crashing down on me, and I have nobody to go to. I need to call Addison and figure this out immediately.

"S.O.S. CALL ME NOW," says the text I sent to Addison.

"I can't talk right now I have a mock trial for my final! If you have an emergency, call Claire. I promise I'll call you later!!!"

That's not a terrible idea actually. I haven't really seen Claire since Thanksgiving when I ran into her at the Macy's parade. She seems friendly, and I feel bad that I haven't really tried to do anything with her. Addison is right, though, she's probably the closest thing to family I have here besides the Quinlan's. I'd call Donald, but I wouldn't want to lead him on. Moving out of their house was hard enough on the two of them. I thought for sure they'd be ready for me to leave but I guess I was the glue to their marriage.

I call Claire and explain my situation without giving too much information away. I want her to know that it's urgent so she would know I need her. We decide on dinner tonight at the sushi place that Chase took me to a couple of months ago. If she's anything like Addison, she will love this place. Hopefully, she can give me some insight into this disaster I have concocted. I knew it was only a matter of time before something went array. Nothing bad has happened to me since I've been in the city besides the news of Hugh being married and that pales in comparison to this issue. My job is what's keeping me in the city to BE with Hugh…

I want to tell Hugh about this, but I know he'll be devastated and probably want to dump me if he finds out. He'll wonder why I didn't tell him when he was so open with me about Emma. I know he'd be more devastated if he finds out from someone other than me. We already have our flights booked for Charleston. Maybe I should just tell him then.

There's no good time. I can't break up with Hugh, and I can't lose my job. I need to figure out a solution so I can keep both.

I can't focus the rest of the afternoon because I really want to solve this fiasco. Claire said she could meet right after work, so that really suited me. I'm not supposed to see Hugh tonight anyways because he has a Christmas party to go to with Elle Magazine at some place Jay-Z and Beyoncé go to apparently. He invited me to go, but I didn't think it was time to announce our relationship to the entire syndicate. I don't really want to bring too much attention to myself, especially right now.

After what seemed like a century of waiting, it's time to meet Claire and get things off my chest. I was able to sneak out of the office without many noticing me. Hugh met me in the lobby so he could walk me to the sushi restaurant around the corner. I tried really hard not to show my emotions, so I put on my best poker face and pretended everything was normal. I get this weird suspicion that he already knows something is wrong. He's really perceptive of my moods and really good at figuring me out.

"Come over later tonight, ok?" He says as he kisses my forehead sweetly.

"I'll try, but I really need to start packing to go home. I'll call you."

I walk in and sit down at a corner table similar to where I sat with

Chase the first time. I look around to make sure I don't recognize anyone from work or God forbid, Emma. I don't know how celebrities ever get to go out to dinner in this city because there's probably someone watching them at all times.

After waiting for nearly twenty-minutes for Claire and drinking two glasses of wine, she finally shows up. She missed the memo that I'm freaking out and need to talk *immediately.*

"I'm so sorry I'm late. I left my laptop in my office and had to go back for it. Did you already order?"

"It's ok-No big deal I'm just panicking. No, I can't eat. I'm just drinking. But feel free."

"You should eat. That's number one on the list. Addison sent me a text telling me you really need someone to talk to. She didn't explain herself, so I figured it was urgent."

"Ok, I'll eat. Let's order a couple of rolls and start figuring out what I'm going to do with this predicament."

Once I'm done explaining my situation, Claire was in awe. First of all, she's surprised that her sister kept that kind of secret from her. Second of all, she thinks I'm kind of screwed, but she has a plan for me. Not one that I really like but it's probably my only option at this point.

"Well, holy shit. You're screwed seven ways to Sunday. You and my sister are never allowed to make decisions under the influence of tequila ever again. My best advice in this kind of situation is to tell the truth. I know it sucks, and it's risky but believe it or not, your boss, Courtney or whoever will probably think it's mature and brave for coming to her with this. Also, this Emma chick is going to screw you seven ways to Sunday regardless."

"You think I should just tell Courtney? And tell Hugh?"

"I didn't say tell Hugh. Deal with Courtney first. If she fires you, it's possible you won't be working in New York ever again, and your relationship will end anyways. Long distance relationships hardly ever work. If Courtney takes it well and you end up keeping your position at the magazine, you have to tell Hugh. I just think you need to cool off first. Figure out a way to tell him that won't ruin the trust between you two."

"Well, that won't be easy because his ex-wife cheated on him and he values trust very much."

"I'm not trying to throw shade at you or anything, but you're dating a guy that's been married and divorced. Surely he'll understand that you had to tell a little lie a little to get a job. You said you hardly ever have to lie to him about college so maybe he'll be ok with it. Just trust your instincts."

"Your advice is really good, Claire. I'm lucky to have you in my life and lucky to have your sister as well. So when and how am I going to approach Courtney?"

"Thanks, Hun, I'm a bit older and wiser. Just call me *Yoda*. I think the sooner you tell her, the better. Send her an email tonight saying you need to meet with her in the morning, and it's urgent. Try, to be honest and not make excuses. It's possible you'll keep your job. I'm not really sure. But I don't see that you have a choice if you want to keep your relationship. I hope this guy is *really* special."

Claire is right. I have to tell Courtney, and I really don't want to. I do feel like I'll enjoy my life a little better knowing that this is off my chest. I also realize that I'll have to tell my roommate. I don't know how she'll react to this. I'm praying she won't throw me out. I hate having to come clean to everyone. I feel like I'm a huge disappointment. I'm just hoping Courtney will be in the holiday spirit and allow me to continue at the magazine.

Godspeed…

Thirty

If you lie you'll steal, if you beg You'll Borrow

I don't know how my life has come to this, but it has. Nothing good ever comes from people lying or stretching the truth. It always comes out in the end whether you hope and wish for it not to. Courtney is able to meet with me in the conference room this morning as long as I brought her an extra hot, light foam, extra drizzle, sugar-free mocha soy latte from Starbucks. I'd bring her one every day for a year if she'd let me keep my job. I take that back-that damn drink cost a fortune.

"What is so important that you needed to be the first face I see today? I hope this latte is extra hot."

"Courtney, I don't know how you'll receive this news, but I truly hope you can have an open mind about it."

"Just tell me. I have an appointment for my dog to be groomed this morning, and I can't be late."

"I didn't go to Columbia."

"Neither did I, what's your point?"

"I mean that I didn't go there, and I put it on my resume. Actually my best friend, Addison did it and sent my resume as a joke. I kept it to myself because I didn't realize it until Nicole mentioned me attending Columbia in my interview. I knew then Addison had sent in a fake resume. I wasn't able to get jobs all summer after graduating, and she thought it would be funny to see what happens if she altered a few things."

"So you mean to tell me you didn't go to college, and you've been one of our top editors that we've hired in the last five years!?"

"I'm one of your top editors?"

"Get to the point, Hanes."

"Of course, I went to college I just didn't go to *Columbia*. I went to College of Charleston where I majored in English and minored in art."

"I see. I can't say I'm happy you were deceptive about this. I will need to talk to Nicole in hiring and Susan in HR. I would hate to see you go because I really think you have potential. I admire you coming forward, but I must ask, why now?"

"Honestly, my boyfriend's ex-wife found out I saved a man's life from this interview she saw on TV two years ago. The man I saved just died and the story resurfaced in the media. She threatened to tell you herself. I know it's crazy, and I should have come forward on my own before now, but I really love it here. I finally feel like I'm doing what I was born to do."

" You saved a man's life? That chick sounds nuts. I'm sorry you've been keeping all of this pinned up. I don't have much time to keep talking about this. I'm going to have to meet with Nicole and Susan, but I should have an answer for you soon. It's not up to me; it's up to them. I will try my best to advocate for you and tell them how well you've thrived here."

"Thank you, Courtney. So much. It feels really good to have this off my chest. I hope they are as understanding as you."

"Don't thank me yet. I'll call you tonight with the answer they give me. They don't really take well to lying, but I will try to figure this mess out for you."

I can't believe the way Courtney reacted. I was afraid she'd throw her latte in my face and tell me to get the hell out. I have to realize it's not like I *pretended* to be someone else. I hope they can see that I didn't do it to advance I just did it to land a job. I know that coming forward during the interview would have been the right thing to do. What I did was wrong, but I'm hoping they will have some mercy on me.

I can't help but feel awful the rest of the day. Hugh took me to lunch, and he noticed I barely ate anything on my plate. I will feel better once the verdict is in but until then I'll just have to tell him I'm sick or something. It's not a total lie; I do feel like I could vomit uncontrollably for the rest of the day.

Once I got home, I start cleaning the entire place from top to bottom. I feel like using this stress for a good cause and putting my energy into something more respectable than binge-watching *Orange is the New Black* for the next three hours and eating raw cake batter. Cabot is in Connecticut visiting her parents, and Hugh thinks I'm coming down with the flu, so I was able to be alone and deal with this by myself. I wait for my phone to ring all night and finally around ten o'clock I get a phone call from Courtney. I'm so scared to pick up because this conversation will make or break my career forever.

"Scarlett, hi, it's Courtney. I have good news and bad news," she said with a serious voice.

Seems like that is what everyone says when there is a predicament like this.

"Ok, just lay it on me."

"I spoke with Nicole and Susan together this evening over dinner. I literally went to dinner with these women on your behalf. You owe me a very expensive bottle of champagne. We all watched the video about you saving the man in Charleston. We think that is incredible and very noble. However, Nicole was hesitant to keep you on, but she read your most recent segments and realized you have too much potential to outright fire you. Susan, being the HR lady, told me every single rule you broke and tried to let you go, but she liked your December issue; she said she could relate or something bizarre. I finally got them to come to a decision."

"Courtney that is so amazing. I don't even know how to thank you for this."

"Don't thank me. Just keep up the good work-a lot of work. We are going to keep you, but you're going to have to write three segments before the break Wednesday since we are nearing Paris Fashion Week. Also, we are going to revoke your pay for this month and take away your holiday bonus."

"That's not going to be easy, but I can do it. I can handle not being paid; I can't handle losing my job. I can't thank you enough."

"You're welcome. I plan on asking you for many favors in the near future. Just be ready."

Courtney's grace during this situation is refreshing. I've been under the impression she hated all the staff, especially me. I'm so happy I could probably run to Times Square and back and have the energy to do it again. I call Claire to thank her for her advice and let her know that I get to keep my job. I decide that I will tell Hugh and my family when we're home for the break...*maybe*. I don't want to stress him out before then since he has deadlines, and now I do too.

Thirty - One

Au Revoir

The best part about telling the truth and coming out to Courtney is being able to tell Emma to suck it. I didn't realize how good it would feel to tell my nemeses how I just *owned it*. I'm banking on her not telling Hugh before our trip, and I'll still have time to figure out a way to break the news to him. I feel like I've never really talked to Hugh about college in depth so it probably won't be that big of a deal. I immediately message Emma at the very last minute today because I wanted her to squirm. I also wanted to see if she'd actually come in our office, which she hasn't-shocker.

> *Dear Emma,*
>
> *I wanted to thank you for coming to me the other day like you did. I came forward to my boss, the hiring manager, and human resources. Turns out I get to keep my job and my boyfriend. If you think you have something over me, you don't. Please do not contact me and leave Hugh the hell alone. He's over you.*
>
> *Merry Christmas! Happy Holidays! Happy Hanukah*
> *Scarlett*

It's somewhat concerning as to what her next move will be, but I don't even care. She can come to Courtney or Nicole or Susan for all I care because they already know. I don't think it will make me look worse. I don't even think Hugh would even believe her crazy ass if she went to *him*. I never even admitted to Emma that she was right about my lie. I just decided to take matters into my own hands. Maybe she was bluffing, and she's not even coming to the city this weekend.

I had plans to go out with Cabot tonight to exchange Christmas presents since she's traveling to the Caribbean all next week until the New Year on her dad's yacht. I figure I will get her liquored up, and tell her the truth. I don't feel right keeping this from her, and I really don't think she'll care.

I spent the rest of this beautiful sunny Friday working on my three segments that Courtney demanded I finish by Wednesday. I'm not sure why she wanted these done so soon I just figured it was probably some form of corporate punishment. I've never been so eager to do work in my life. I'm thankful to have all this work piled on me at once. It's a good distraction, and it's allowing me to keep my job. I want these three pieces to be the best writing I've ever done. I'm going to prove to this company that I'm worthy of working here.

Friday night in New York City during the holiday season is like a jungle trying to get around all these insane people. I never thought I'd be annoyed with tourist since I just moved here not too long ago but I'm starting to really feel like a local at this point.

Cabot wants to go to some upscale bar with expensive martinis and Wall Street executives. She said she wanted to start scoping out the scene to look for a wealthy bachelor. She tells me she's not a gold-digger, she just knows that having money makes things easier, and they are usually much smarter than the ones with no money. She might have a point there.

We finally got to the bar after sharing a cab from work. It seems that everyone goes out after work for drinks because they need time to decompress from their stressful day. I've started to become a nightly drinker since I've moved here. One or two glass of red wine aren't so bad; it's good for your heart after all. Doctors say that drinking one glass of wine is equivalent to an hour in the gym, so I'm basically a gym rat now.

I realized that I'm going to have to take it easy on the spending since I won't be getting a paycheck this month. It really sucks, but it's better than three months without pay or even longer. Hell, it's better than not having a job at all. I was able to save a good bit when I lived with Lisa and Donald. If I really want some extra money I could probably sell my watch and my earrings that Donald gave me. It's not a terrible idea except that it is since I *love* them.

This is the kind of bar that you expect all the guys here to buy you drinks but they don't. Instead, they all stand in huddles with their expensive suits on and their expensive bourbon drinks trying to look all sophisticated and what not. All of these guys look to be around thirty or so. Could be the receding hairlines and the dumb comb-over look. This is the kind of bar Donald probably came to with his finance buddies. I seriously wonder how he's doing since the split probably off buying expensive jewelry for other women.

"Do you want to get a table or just sit here at the bar?" Cabot said as she sipped her fancy pomegranate martini.

"This is fine if you're good. How was your day?"

"I'm slammed at work. I'm trying to get my writing turned in before everyone else does so I can have an edge."

"What are you referring to? What writing?"

I'm curious now as to what she's talking about. We usually don't talk about work stuff. "Didn't Courtney tell you? Hearst is sending one person from each magazine to Paris Fashion Week in February on a twelve-week all-expense paid trip. They are choosing the candidates Tuesday before the break. I'm hoping one of them will be good enough to get chosen."

"What?! That's awesome. Why didn't I know about this?"

Of course, I'm not supposed to know about this. Courtney wants me to write these segments but not tell me to do my very best. She wants to see what effort I'll go to in order to keep my job. She probably doesn't want to tell me that I'll get rewarded with a trip to Paris if I'm chosen.

"Yep. I've never been to Paris this is a dream of mine. I think I have a good shot at it. Are you going to submit?"

Why would Courtney have me writing three segments due Wednesday, the same date as the contest? She probably wants me to win so everyone will hate me. Her niceness towards me has a motive.

"Wow. Well, good luck with that. I wasn't actually told about this contest…Courtney is making me do the three articles regardless."

"Why? It's voluntary."

"Well, that's why I brought you here. I have to tell you something. Remember how I told you I'm from Charleston? Well. I lied."

"You're not from Charleston?"

"No-let meant to finish. I'm from Charleston. I went to College of Charleston."

"So? I knew that…"

"You did?! How did you know?"

"Your mom told me that day we went out for brunch. I guess you were in the bathroom or something. How is that a lie, though?"

"Oh, I didn't know she did that. Now I feel stupid telling you this, but I guess I should tell you anyways. I lied on my resume."

"How so?"

She's now being really short with me. I can tell she's about to be upset. I explained to her what Addison did and how it landed me in NYC.

"Umm..what? So now you're being forced to enter this contest for Paris, and you don't even deserve it?"

"Courtney didn't really give me a choice, and she didn't tell me about the contest. I'm so sorry Cabot. I really am."

"You know this isn't fair right? Like, I really want to win, and I'm working hard to do so. I can't believe you lied!"

"I know it's not fair. Technically I never really told you where I went to school. I wasn't lying I was just being deceptive with you and I'm really sorry."

"I need to go home. I'm going to have to work extra hard now since you're going to win by default. You made junior editor before anyone at work. Maybe you should sleep at Hugh's tonight."

I don't really want to stay at Hugh's because I'm upset, and he's seen me frazzled all week. I can't tell him yet, or it will ruin our Christmas and our New Years. I hate that I upset Cabot, but I can't really help it. I must say-she took it better than I anticipated. She gave me a lot of attitude, and made some pretty crass accusations, but she will get over it. If I do win the contest, she'll probably be looking for a new roommate.

Thirty - Two

All I want for Christmas

Things were pretty frosty between Cabot and me until today the day before she left for the Caribbean. We finally made peace with each other and exchanged gifts. She thought it would be funny to give me all Columbia paraphernalia. It was kind of nice that she broke the ice about the situation on Friday night. We hardly spoke to each other all weekend. I decided to give her my precious robin's egg blue box with the Tiffany's earrings because I felt bad that I lied, and I really didn't have the money to get her an actual gift right now. She was shocked and so excited that she decided to let things go. She even told me she would possibly be happy if I won the contest.

Sunday became a day we did almost everything together; from breakfast to dinner we were inseparable. I'm really sad that I have to spend the next couple of days in our apartment alone. Hugh and I picked out a small tree yesterday, and we put some white lights on it. I told him that my grandparents would have all the Christmas décor up to make it feel more like the holidays. My grandmother has probably had everything up since the day after Thanksgiving. I'm really excited for him to meet my family.

Cabot left for the airport early Monday morning before I was ready for work. She came in to wake me up and tell me Merry Christmas and that she hopes I have a great break even though I'll be broke and she'll be the one getting tan and sipping mango daiquiris. She wanted to rub it in my face that I won't be getting paid. She's still a little bitter about everything. I think she secretly feels that I'm a good contender for this contest.

I didn't have much to do at work today except sit at my desk and re-format my articles. I decided to write something from the heart; something that really speaks to me- a piece about moving from your hometown on the southern coast to a big city. I wrote my other two about fashion trends from 2015 and wedding planning. That last one might be due to all the pinning I've done Pinterest for my future wedding.

I figured one of them would win the judge over. I'm not sure who was going to be choosing the candidate because technically I wasn't supposed to know that I was entering a contest. I still can't figure out why Courtney wouldn't just tell me upfront.

I did some research on Paris Fashion Week, and it looks like it actually falls on the week of my birthday. What an amazing trip that would be if I did get it; I wondered if Hugh was entering his photos into the contest. I text him to meet me in the coffee room even though I know he'll be there since it's *that* time of day.

"Hey baby, did you enter this Paris contest? I forgot to ask you this weekend. We were distracted if you know what I mean."

"I did. They do this every year here at Hearst. I love Paris. I would *love* to take you there someday."

He is such a romantic. I don't know how I got so lucky with this guy.

"Well, I entered the contest as well. Maybe we will get to go sooner than you think."

"That would be amazing. I would *love* that."

"I *love* you."

I slipped. I didn't even mean to say that. I didn't realize that I loved him like *this,* but I guess I do. I'm afraid to know what he'll say to this.

"That's a surprise…I don't know what to say, Scar," he says as he fills his coffee with more sugar than normal.

"I'm sorry. I didn't mean to just blurt that out. Emotions have been running high, and I haven't had much sleep."

"So you *don't* love me? Is that what you're saying?"

"No! I do! But you didn't say it back…"

"I was hoping to tell you when we got to your parents. I was going to surprise you and make it really special. Something you deserve."

"I am so sorry that I ruined it for you. I feel like an idiot."

"An idiot that I'm in *love* with"

I've been thinking about this moment for a few weeks now. I've never really been in love with a guy until Hugh. I'm *so* happy that his feelings are reciprocated, and he didn't wait to make some grand gesture to tell me. It just feels more natural this way. I don't even care if I win this stupid contest. I'm just so happy that my boyfriend feels this way about me. I still feel conflicted that I haven't told him what's been going on in my life. Claire did tell me to wait until the right time. I really don't feel like there's ever going to be a *"right time"* but I will tell him soon.

I think it's best I turn my writing into Courtney early; that way she could see I'm serious about my work. I want her to know that I'm willing to rewrite them if she hates them. I would do anything to keep my job because keeping my job meant staying in the city where my *love* is.

She accepts them and tells me that she's happy I was able to complete the task on time. She didn't mention the contest, so it's possible she just wanted me to do the same amount of work everyone was doing. Scrambling around to get things done like a chicken with their head cut off. She probably knew that I'd notice everyone else hammering out pages, so she wanted me to have the same workload.

Cabot has been sending me pictures of her on this incredible yacht all night, and it's really distracting me. I've been attempting to pack for our trip to Charleston hoping that the next twenty-four hours will fly. The past few days have been nothing but surfing the Internet for the perfect Christmas gift for Hugh. I don't really want to buy him a gift as much as I wanted to give him the perfect holiday. I know he doesn't care about what I give him; I have a feeling whatever he gets me, he will top my idea anyways. He's been subtly asking me for weeks what I want. I kept trying to emphasize that I don't need anything, and he's *all* I want for Christmas.

I promised Cabot that I would keep her informed about the contest. She didn't have Wi-Fi, just some burner phone on the boat so I told her to call me tomorrow around lunch when they're announcing the winner. I wasn't supposed to know this, but obviously, she knew all the details. I'm surprised that she left for vacation at a time like this but she said she's tried to win this contest since she started working there and she hasn't been able to. You would think you'd eventually just give up after not winning three years in a row. That's nine grueling segments and countless hours of hard work to possibly get rejected once again. She must really want to go to Paris. With her kind of money, frankly I'm surprised that she hasn't already gone. I will *sort of* feel bad if I win the contest, and I wasn't even trying to. I haven't had a burning desire to go to Europe, but I guess it would be really romantic if Hugh got to go with me.

Thirty - Three

Two-Faced B!$#*

Lately, I've been really stressed out with the craziness of Emma and coming to Courtney about my issues. Finally, things are becoming normal again, and I don't feel as stressed out. I'm suddenly very nervous about this contest announcement. My gut tells me this is unfair and cruel to my roommate and someone I'm now considering to be one of my best friends, but I can't help but get excited to know the winner.

Courtney calls all the editors to the middle of the office to make a big announcement. I already knew what she was about to tell us.

"I know all of you have been *eagerly* waiting for this moment. There are many of you who deserve this trip to Paris, but only one of you can represent Cosmopolitan. I'm excited to announce that this year's winner of the fashion week contest is, Scarlett Hanes, one of our newest members to the company."

"What? Me? Are you kidding?"

I look at Courtney with disbelief and try to pretend I had no idea what she was talking about. Everyone was clapping, but they all looked pissed and went back to their desk.

"I didn't want to tell you because then you'd know you'd be

rewarded for work I thought you needed to do regardless of the trip to Paris. I hope this means you will learn to tell the truth and never betray our trust again. We like you, Scarlett." she said in a whisper so that nobody would hear.

The amount of *ticked off* faces around the office is at an all-time high. I didn't realize this is such a big deal to everyone. I really feel like this is some form of punishment so that nobody will like me here.

"Thank you, Courtney. I won't ever let you down again. I just have one favor to ask."

"I don't think you're really in the position to be asking favors but go ahead."

"Do you think you could send Cabot Vanderbilt in my place? She really worked hard to win this, and I don't deserve it."

"Oh no, honey. You're going, and you're personally going to tell Cabot that you won. You see, I know Cabot is your roommate. I know you're becoming close. I also know that it's her dream to win this trip. You deserve this. You deserve to have to tell her after the stunt you pulled."

"Do you mean that I deserve to have my friendship ruined?"

"I didn't say that. Don't put words in my mouth. But I will say that it's only fair that you have to be the one to break it to her. Winning this trip might bring on a lot of enemies. Life's a bitch isn't it?"

All this time I thought Courtney was trying to be nice to me. Turns out she is a conniving, two-faced bitch who knew what she was doing from the time I told her about my resume situation. I knew it was too good to be true that I was able to keep my job. She wants me to be the one everyone loathes in the office for being the girl who comes in here and wins the biggest contest of the year. She wants everyone to hate me. Well done, Courtney. Everyone *is* going to hate me if they don't already.

I can't think of a way to tell Cabot the news. I feel so conflicted about it. I've written down what I'm going to say to her a thousand times on at least ten different sticky notes. I break down and call her on the way back from lunch, and she takes it better than I expected. She cried hysterically for the first few minutes of our conversation, but that was expected because she's quite theatrical on a normal day. She decided that she's too drunk on rum to care, and she would just come on her own accord. I'm relieved, and excited to think we'd get to go together. I'm hoping she still feels this way when she gets home from paradise, or I'm screwed.

I spent the rest of the day on Google maps touring around Paris. I want to see what it looks like and get an idea of the *city of love*. I researched Paris Fashion Week and hadn't realized how big of a deal this is until now. This will be the highlight of my *new* resume. I don't have to lie anymore. I can finally be my authentic self now. My resume will be a thousand times better than my fabricated one. I can't wait to tell my family the news and Addison and Claire. I will wait to tell them in person to see the reaction on their faces.

Now to tell the news to Hugh, I just hope this is an easier conversation with no tears involved.

"I *won* the trip to Paris…" I said as I pulled him closer to me on the couch.

"Funny you should mention that. I actually did too. Looks like we will be kissing under the Eiffel Tower together on your birthday."

"That's so amazing!!! I'm excited. How'd you know it was my

birthday that week?"

"Because I'm your *boyfriend*, and I know these things. Also because I asked Cabot to ask your mom," he said with a chuckle.

"You are one sly guy, you know. I can't believe I'm in love with a guy that I don't even know their birthday!"

"It's in September. So don't worry, you had a while to find out."

"Good. You're a hard guy to find a gift for so that will give me plenty of time to find something."

"You don't have to get me anything. You make me happy, and you're all I need."

"You are so sexy did you know that?" I say as I kiss on his neck and suggest that we turn on the *fire*-in more than one way.

"Likewise my Love."

Hugh put the blanket on the floor in front of the fire. One thing led to another, and we were completely undressed and rolling around in front of the Christmas tree being young and carefree. I'm with the man I adore, we're going home for Christmas tomorrow, and we're going to Paris together in a couple of months. All is right in my world.

Thirty - Four

No Good Deed Goes Unpunished

"It's time to go! We are going to be late if we don't hurry up. Put your clothes on and grab your suitcase," I said as we got out of the shower together.

Our flight is leaving today at noon, and we're still at Hugh's penthouse. We need to be there a good hour and a half early to check in and check our bags. I have become a crazy lady trying to make sure everything is perfect.

"Calm down, Love. We will get there on time. I arranged for a car to take us to LaGuardia."

I should've known that Hugh was going to handle things. He always knows the way to calm me down when I'm frantic. I'm a little nervous as to how everyone will receive him at home, but I have no idea why. He's literally the perfect guy, and I don't deserve him. I keep thinking in the back of my mind that he's going to leave me because I'm not good enough or because he's bored with me. I have this reoccurring dream that he dumps me and goes back to his psycho ex, Emma, and they move to Australia. I think what she did to me a couple of weeks ago put a serious strain on my capacity to trust people. Courtney sort of threw a wrench at me as well so all together I'm a bit messed up from it.

This is the first time we've been at an airport together since we met.

If you would've told me then that we'd be in love and going home for the Christmas break together, I would've told you that you were on drugs. I can't believe this is happening right now. Hugh even booked our tickets as part of my gift. I've never flown first class, but I could certainly get used to this.

"Would you like champagne, Miss?" said the flight attendant who was getting starry-eyed over Hugh and his good looks.

"Yes, please."

I want to tell her to stop staring, but I had to think of it as a compliment. I know he's hot and has an accent that would make any woman weak. I think that's why so many women feel that they can't date him. They don't feel they can trust a man this wonderful, so they just avoid trying. I must have a high self-esteem because I can handle his manly wonderfulness and I trust him fully.

The non-stop flight landed us in Charleston around two o'clock in the afternoon. We wait for our bags for a while, and we both couldn't believe how small the airport seemed compared to the ones in NYC. I feel like everything is so laid back and relaxed too. Everyone is so friendly here and greeted us with smiles and niceties. I can tell that Hugh likes it here because he's been smiling since we landed. I guess he feels more at home being so close to the ocean.

"Have I told you how happy I am to be here with you? Because I am. I'm really excited to spend the holiday with my babe," Hugh said as he pulled me in for one last kiss before seeing the family.

"You don't even know!"

Speaking of family, I kept looking to the exit to see if I could spot my mom's car. She isn't here yet, but I knew I told her what time to come. It's Christmas Eve, so I'm sure that the bridge is just backed up from all the people trying to get home early to be with their family.

"Scarlett!!! Oh my God! I didn't know you were coming in right now!"

I couldn't believe it, but it was Addison squealing from across the conveyer belt. I left Hugh without even explaining myself and ran to my best friend. How could I not?

"SHUT UP! I am so freaking excited to see you!! I can't believe you're here at the same time as us."

"Us?"

"Surprise!!! I brought my boyfriend home with me for Christmas."

"Get out. Is he that hot guy you were standing next to that looks like he should be in a movie or something?"

"Yes   *guilty*"

"Get out of here…you better introduce me!"

I walk Addison over to where Hugh is picking up our bags that finally came around. He's super polite as expected and gives her a huge hug picking her off the ground when doing so. She practically demanded it. I can tell she approves because she asked him a thousand questions about Australia and when can she expect us to get married. She's a bit jacked up from all the caffeine she had on her flight. They should make people show their ID for espresso these days. It's lethal.

My mom finally made it to the airport and brought my sister with her. Savannah is clearly in shock of how handsome Hugh is and how amazingly kind he is; similar to Addison's reaction but with less pestering questions. I can tell my sister is crushing over him because every time he'd ask her a question she would blush and stutter. He seems really happy here and genuinely glad to be with my family and me.

"I hope you two are hungry because your grandmother has been in the kitchen the past couple of days preparing for our dinner tonight," said my mom as she turned onto our street.

I'm getting so excited to be home in my bedroom where everything is so *normal* and so right.

"We are quite ready for the holiday feast, Ms. Riley," Hugh said as he reassured her we are happy to be home.

"Please, call me Kate," my mom says while trying not to get overly excited about his accent.

I have a feeling this is going to be everyone's reaction. Nobody in Charleston will expect me to be dating a super-hot Aussie. I can't wait to *parade* him around town. I'm hoping I will run into some of the haters I went to school with around town.

We spent the afternoon resting and getting changed for church service and dinner with the entire family. My dad is even bringing Naomi over because apparently her and my mother are trying to be on better terms. My grandparents weren't exactly approving of their arrangement but since its Christmas they said they would let it slide. I'm not exactly thrilled about her intruding on our family holiday but in the spirit of Christmas, I'll just ignore her and drink more wine to tolerate it. She makes my dad happy, so that's all that matters I suppose.

"This is such a lovely estate you have, Mrs. Riley, thank you so much for hosting us tonight," Hugh says as he walks in the front door of my grandparent's house for dinner.

He was quiet at church and seemed a bit out of place. We weren't able to introduce Hugh to my grandparents until after the service since we were late getting there due to us getting into the eggnog a little too early.

"You are so very welcome my dear. We're glad to have you spend the holiday with us. We've missed our darling Scarlett terribly."

Everything is decorated impeccably just as I suspected it would be. The entire house smelled of fresh Balsam and Frasier fir. The Christmas village is set up in the living room, and there's garland and lights hanging everywhere; Christmas music playing, everyone is standing around drinking, talking and having a great time. My family knows how to put on a Christmas party.

I feel a sense of sadness while watching everyone enjoying themselves. It's Christmas Eve, and I still haven't told Hugh about everything. I think I'm most afraid he'll be mad for keeping this from him for so long when I've had every opportunity to dish out the details. I don't want to start the New Year with this looming over my head. I need to tell him now, or I'll never tell him.

"I'd like to propose a toast: As you all know, I'm so very happy to be here with you to celebrate Christmas. I've been waiting a long time to be home and see all of your beautiful faces. Thank you so much for having us. I'm especially happy to have here with me, Hugh, my love. I know the timing of this announcement may be sudden, but I can't wait any longer."

I couldn't help but look sad and disappointed. I lowered my head and couldn't make eye contact with anyone. Everyone is silent.

"What is it Scarlett, darling? What's wrong?" My grandfather said as he came near me to embrace me with a hug in support of my sadness.

I broke out in tears; I can't believe I decided this is the moment to break everyone's hearts.

"I didn't want to tell any of you, *ever*. I feel like I can't enjoy Christmas with this looming over my conscience."

I told them everything. I literally can't stop balling. I'm devastated in how they reacted. Nobody would even look at me: except Hugh.

"Can we please go outside and talk a bit?"

We left the *very* quiet room of *very* disappointed family members. I'm so ashamed of myself.

"Sure. I am SO sorry, Hugh. I really am."

"Why haven't you told me this yet? I'm so embarrassed that you couldn't have the decency to tell me in private. Now your entire family knows, and I feel ridiculous. I don't even know what to say to you right now except how can I trust you?"

The sheer anger, and disappointment in his voice is something I've never experienced until now; things were great, and I just ruined it.

"I know the timing of it is bad. I had no choice. I was going to be sick if I waited any longer. I wanted to tell you so many times. Emma scared me. I was afraid she'd tell you before I could get the chance. I wanted to tell you the night you told me about your divorce but I couldn't. I just haven't found the right time."

"So you chose now? On Christmas Eve?"

"I know. I feel awful about it. Everyone probably hates me now for ruining their night."

"Nobody hates you. Especially me. But I do feel like I need some time to think about this. I put my trust in you."

"You lied to me *too* if you don't recall. The night on the rooftop you had plenty of opportunities to tell me you were MARRIED!"

"Don't spin this on me. I know I messed up but I confessed everything to you."

"I know. I'm sorry. I don't know what else to do to make this right."

"I just need a *little* time. I feel like I should just go."

"You can't spend Christmas alone! Please don't leave! Please!"

"Just tell your family I had to go back; they will understand."

"I don't want you to leave. I want you to stay. Please understand I didn't mean to hurt you!"

"I know you didn't mean to. I trusted you. I told you I *love* you. I don't just throw that word around, Scarlett."

"Nothing has changed. I love you and I mean it."

"I love you. But right now I do *not* like you. I feel stupid."

"If you leave it will ruin things between us. Please stay."

"I can't. I'll see you when we get back. Please tell your family thank you for having me."

"So that's it? Are you *breaking* up with me?"

"I just need to be alone right now, Scarlett."

"I'm sorry. I really am. I wish you'd reconsider staying. They don't think you're a fool! I would never hurt you on purpose. Ever."

The tears keep flowing. I can't stop crying. He got in a cab and went away. I didn't try to race after him. This isn't a movie. This is real. I can't make this right. I need to figure out a way to straighten this mess out. I didn't expect him to be so upset with me. I've never seen him this way.

My world just came crashing down on me. In the blink of an eye, everything we had is destroyed. My family feels so bad for me that they aren't even mad. I know they're disappointed in me, which is worse but they tried so hard to console me. Even Naomi was sympathetic in her own weird way. I have to make this right. I have to figure out a way to get Hugh back. I need him to trust me.

"Honey, you better GET in the car and go find him. He's a catch. He didn't deserve you dropping that bomb on him like that in front of all of us you should've waited to tell him in private," said my dad who is seriously upset with me right now.

"I don't know where to go. I don't know where he went."

"I would start by going back to Daniel Island. He can't just leave all his stuff here."

"Ok. I've been drinking, though. I need someone to drive me."

"I'll take you. I'm on call tonight, so I'm stone cold sober. Let's go get your man *back*."

"Thanks, daddy."

"You can't let this guy slip away. I can see that there's something special between you two. You can't deny that kind of love. Hell, I think he's good looking!"

"You're right. It is special. I think he's the *one*."

"Well, we better drive *fast* then."

My dad and I get in the car and rush to the island as fast as we can since my dad has the cop car tonight. He put the siren on, and we got there in fifteen minutes, which is nearly a record time from downtown. I run in the door of my house and find Hugh sitting at the kitchen table drinking vodka straight from the bottle. I guess I've driven him to this.

"Oh my God. Thank you! You're still here," I said as I run up to the kitchen table and sit next to him. My mascara is running down my face, and I look like a total nut job, but I don't care.

"What are you doing?" He said as he stood up from the table.

"I came to tell you to *stay*! That I'm madly in love with you, and I made a *huge* mistake not telling you from the very beginning the truth about things! Everyone makes mistakes. I made a *big* one. I know you trusted me, and I'll have to regain your trust somehow but I would do *anything* to keep you here and to forgive me."

"Scarlett, I wasn't going back to the city tonight. I told you I needed some *space*, some time to think. That's why I came here. I don't exactly know my way around Charleston. I just knew your address and thought I would see you later tonight."

"What? I thought you were going back to the city?!"

"Of course not. I meant what I said when I told you I *love* you. I am IN *love* with you. I just felt like I needed to get away from everybody. I feel like a fool being the last one to know things."

"*I'm so sorry*, babe! I promise they don't think you're a fool. They think you're *amazing*. Literally the opposite of a fool-the best guy ever."

"It's ok I guess. I know I betrayed your trust before, and you were really forgiving. I only wish you knew you could've leaned on me in a time like this. I would have embraced you. That's the main reason I felt so frustrated. I would do anything for you and this little white lie or whatever isn't going to stop me from feeling the way I do about you. "

"I should have leaned on you. I'm a big dumb idiot. I don't even know how I got myself into this craziness. Well-I do, but it's just weird how I let it change me.

"I think I can let it slide this one time. I just want to get things back to how they were as fast as possible," Hugh says as he pulls my waist into his body.

"I wish this night could end the way that one night did; minus all the whip cream that *ruined* my new dress."

"Maybe it can; for the sake of Christmas. We'll have a lot of time to make up for our mistakes later. For now, we should just move on and deal with it when we get back to the city. No whip cream next time," he said as he pulled me in for a hug and a kiss.

"*Deal.*"

Acknowledgements

When I was three, my mom and dad asked me what I wanted to be when I grew up. My response was always: "an ice cream truck," yes the *literal* truck, but they knew what I meant obviously. I wanted to make people happy. And eat all the free ice cream possible. Can you blame me? I never in a million years pictured myself as a published author. I just hope I can make my readers as happy as I wanted to as the ice cream "truck." I have a laundry list of people who helped make this happen. When they say, "It takes a village," they ain't lyin! Here it goes:

It sounds very trite to thank my parents profusely, but without them, I wouldn't have had the education I did growing up. I'm eternally grateful for your constant love and support. My parents started teaching me to read and to know the meaning of words at the age of two. Partly because my big brother, Michael was learning so I wanted to as well.

Mom, you are my rock! I can't imagine this novel without your never-ending ideas and knowledge of the low country. Your personality shows through in my writing quite often, and if you know my mom you'll understand why I say that. I can't wait until the day I read your book-thank you for inspiring me. The determination to finish what I started has always been something you've instilled in me from such a young age. I appreciate you never letting me give up. Except soccer, *thank you* for letting me quit.

You too dad; I know I get my competitive nature from you, and I think it's something to admire. Your encouragement and enthusiasm is something I cherish. You are always giving me advice on how to spin things into a positive situation no matter what. Your positivity is contagious and I love you for it. I know you'll always support me in whatever I do. (Within reason) Your reaction to me pursuing writing was really important to me. I always want to make you feel proud, and you truly did when I told you the release date of Pink Lies.

A huge thank-you to my husband's cousin and my friend, Best Selling Author, Stacey Lynn: I swear I wouldn't be publishing this book for another five years if you hadn't helped so much along the way. Your passion and insight inspired me to pull this off. I appreciate you mentoring me and not losing it when I asked fifty questions to only figure it out myself five minutes later.

Chloe, thank you for using your inner nerd to be a beta reader and for being a true book worm. Good Reads member since 6th grade!! I appreciate it!!

Meg, thank you for being my Meg. For helping inspire the title of this novel. I don't know what I'd do without our forever friendship!

Also, my bestie from college whom I adore, Mary Elizabeth-your enthusiasm to read my novel and get excited for me was the best gift you could ever given me. This world is a lot better with your bright personality and never ending kindness. Thank you for all the late nights of reading. Sorry for the hangovers, I can't help my book is one to be consumed with vino!

I can't forget my very talented illustrator, Victoria Blanchard. What would I do without you? I can't draw. Let's be honest: my idea was a bit unconventional, but you made it happen. I appreciate your patience and your willingness to make my unique vision come to life. Also, you're a great friend and an impeccable listener. Thanks for always being honest and keeping it real with me.

A special thanks to my inner circle of friends that helped support this venue from the very beginning until the end. I appreciate you more than you know. Having amazing people like you in my life to make me feel loved is something I truly cherish.

Last, but not least, the sweetest man in the universe: my husband, Marcus Kitts. Your love and support during the inception of this novel is unparalleled to anything I've *ever* seen on any romantic chick flick. You are the real deal, honey. I appreciate you allowing me to get up in the middle of the night to write or edit; to allow Scarlett Hanes into our home life. To be the shoulder, I cry on when I forgot to save my work and not letting me shave my head in rage because of it. You have more patience than anyone I know. And you're handsome as hell. So thanks for being easy on the eyes and charming. I love you. <u>So much</u>!

About the Author

Haley Kitts graduated from East Carolina University with a B.S. In Communication and Public Relations where she developed a love for words and writing. She then spent time abroad in France eating croissants and drinking espresso while watching her husband play professional basketball. She loves watching Ina Garten & Bobby Flay and cooking the marvelous food they share on their shows. Haley lives in Raleigh, North Carolina where she grew up visiting Wrightsville Beach many times; playing in the sand, surfing, wakeboarding, eventually getting married there in 2014.

Website: www.haleytoddkitts.com
Facebook: www.facebook.com/HaleyToddKittsAuthor
Instagram: www.instagram.com/label_me_hales/

Thank you for entering Scarlett's world in Pink Lies. I hope you will take the journey to Paris with the Southern Belle and her Aussie to see where their love story ends up.

-Haley Todd Kitts, Author of Pink Lies & Pink Lies in Paris

Read on for an excerpt from

Pink Lies in Paris

by Haley Todd Kitts

-A Sneak Peak of Pink Lies in Paris-

As you know by now, I have a terrible time organizing for a major trip. Since moving in with, Hugh, I at least have a much larger closet for all my belongings. My grandparents aren't thrilled with the idea of me "living in sin" but they should be happy that I'm trying to be practical. I'll never get ahead in this city unless I save every penny I can. Cabot was actually very understanding when I told her I was moving out because I live in the same building as my boyfriend, and I can't see paying the astronomical price of rent when he's only an elevator ride away. She was able to sublet my room to our friend Cooper, one of the graphic designers at Cosmo. I'm not going to lie they're a match made in heaven. Cooper appreciates the Kate Spade China way more than I ever could.

Packing is literally the bane of my existence. Paris is only three days away, and I still have yet to figure out what to bring. With so many events to attend, I'm lucky Cosmo gave me a hefty wardrobe allowance or I'd be wearing my senior prom dress that I got at the Citadel Mall. There are so many times I'd rather be a guy; right now is one of those times. Hugh finished all his laundry and packed his clothes into what I like to call a thimble. When you don't wear any color, you don't have to pack as many clothes. I've been dating him for months and still can't figure out if he's repeated an outfit yet. My main issue is wanting to pack every cute pair of shoes that I own and not being able to decide which are going in the "no" pile. My mother suggested I buy some scarves and tall black boots, so I don't look like a tourist. Truth is, I am a tourist. I don't even care. You will find me wearing my Converse and my consignment shop clothing on the streets of Paris. I have a thing about comfort before being fashionable. Seems like an oxymoron considering I work in the fashion segment of Cosmopolitan Magazine.

"Do you think if we went for a walk and came back you could clear your head and focus on packing tonight," Hugh asked in such a tender loving way as he poured my chai tea into my favorite mug.

"I don't think you understand." Taking slow sips of my warm cardamom tasting drink hoping he will just let it go. "I can't focus on anything but getting this done before tomorrow."

"I think it's much like studying for a very important test, my love. You must take a break to give your brain some rest," Hugh says as he kisses my forehead like he always does when he's consoling me.

"If it will make you happy to go on a walk, I will. As long as some kind of dessert is involved."

You'd think after drinking this sugary chai tea that I wouldn't need a dessert-or the fact that I'm about to live in Paris for the next three months where the pastries are more than abundant.

"I think I can make that happen, how about some cupcakes from Magnolia Bakery?"

"I can't argue with that."

Once we make it back from our long walk to Magnolia's, I decide it's time to phone a friend; my best friend. Addison is going into her second semester of Georgetown Law right now, and she never has any time for me anymore. I want her to soak up these last few days of being in the same time zone because once I'm in France- she'll never have a chance. I don't think she'd appreciate me video chatting her at six in the morning or one in the morning for that matter. She says that she gets a Spring break, and she's considering coming to Paris to spend a week with me. Do I think that will happen? Hell no. But it's worth getting excited about.

"Are you and Hugh going to live in a flat that has a view of the Eiffel Tower?" Addison asks presumptuously.

"I don't think Cosmo wants us *shacking* up in Paris together. I'm not really sure what our living arrangements will be, but I doubt we will have a ten million dollar view."

"Don't you think they can afford it? Geez," Addison said annoyed.

"You would think that, wouldn't you?

"Absolutely, yeah, I would. Hopefully, you'll have some time for yourself and won't be working the entire time."

"I know that wherever I am in France, as long as I have access to a warm room with Wi-Fi, I'll be a happy girl."

"Amen to that."

Made in the USA
Lexington, KY
29 July 2016